Hidden in Her Heart

AN INSPIRATIONAL ROMANCE

Milla Holt

REINBOK LIMITED

London, United Kingdom

Published by Reinbok Limited, 111 Wolsey Drive, Kingston Upon Thames, Greater London, KT2 5DR

Publisher's Note: This is a work of fiction. Names, characters, places, and incidents are a product of the author's imagination. Locales and public names are sometimes used for atmospheric purposes. Any resemblance to actual people, living or dead, or to businesses, companies, events, institutions, or locales is completely coincidental.

Cover by 100Covers

Editing by Krista Wagner

Hidden In Her Heart/ Milla Holt. -- 1st ed.

ISBN 978-1-913416-07-2
Print ISBN 978-1-913416-08-9

To my amazing husband, who is my number one cheerleader and my beta readers Vickie, MaryAnn, Rose, Shantal, and the Hidden Gems duo. Your help was invaluable.

contents

Chapter One

EDEN TRACEY rearranged the canapés on the sterling silver serving tray. "I shouldn't have come," she muttered. The hors d'oeuvres were already perfect. Fiddling with them was just an excuse to avoid going back into the living room. There was only so much time she could hide in the kitchen. She took a step back and eyeballed the tray, then tilted each miniature pastry bite a few millimeters to the left. Things

out there might be awkward and scary, but she could control this tray of food and make it faultless.

"Oh, there you are!"

Eden straightened up, jostling the tray and sending the canapés skittering out of their precisely angled rows into an untidy jumble.

Geoff Gallagher smiled at her from his kitchen doorway, his gray eyes lighting up. He walked up to her and glanced at the trays. "Those look amazing. I'll grab one and we'll go back in. Everyone's eager to know you. Wait a second." He reached toward her and tucked back a lock of black hair that had slipped out of her loose chignon. "There. Come on, let's go."

Guilt gnawed at Eden's conscience, settling into her gut like a dark writhing mass. Geoff had invited her to his place to meet his friends, but she wished she'd made an excuse and stayed home. She didn't know what he had told all these people about their relationship. In fact, she and Geoff had never actually defined what they were to each other.

He was a silent partner in the videography business she ran with his sister, and she'd drifted into the habit of seeing him a couple of times a month. She supposed their outings could technically be called dates, but she hesitated to go as far as saying he was her boyfriend. And then he'd asked her to help him host a dinner party for his closest friends, and she hadn't known how to turn him down or back out of it.

All eyes turned to her as she followed Geoff back into the living room, gripping her tray of canapés.

As soon as she'd arrived here tonight and seen the suppressed eagerness on his friends' faces, she'd known it was a mistake to come. Things had moved on to a much more serious level than she wanted. Didn't all the magazine articles say a guy must be keen on you if he wanted you to meet his best friends? Geoff definitely seemed keen on her, and he was a great guy. But the closer he tried to get, the more uneasy she was. And now she was probably leading him on without meaning to. But how do you dump a guy who isn't officially your boyfriend?

She held the tray toward a woman in a dark blue evening suit who had introduced herself as Beverley. Beverley smiled as she reached out for an hors d'oeuvre. "I really shouldn't because I'm trying to cut down on carbs, but those pastries look absolutely divine."

Geoff spoke from across the room where he was topping off everyone's drinks from a jug of cinnamon-laced fruit punch. "Eden made those herself. Trust me, they're incredible."

"Then I've definitely got to try one." Beverley popped one into her mouth and moaned, rolling her eyes heavenward. "These are divine."

The other guests made similar reactions as they helped themselves to the canapés. Beverley's husband—was he Fred or Frank?—jabbed a long, bejeweled finger toward Eden. "You have got to give me the recipe for these. Where did you learn to cook like this? These are restaurant quality."

Eden set the tray onto the coffee table and smiled at the compliment. "Thank you. Cooking is a hobby. I find it really relaxing."

Beverley snagged another canapé. "I find it relaxing, too, but more often than not I end up scorching everything."

Everyone chuckled, and Fred—or Frank—elbowed Beverley gently. "Oh, the stories I could tell."

The chatter continued as Eden sat down on the edge of an armchair, willing her tense muscles to relax. There was no need to get worked up. She'd said nothing to give Geoff

the idea they were romantically involved, and she could make it clear
to these people that they were just
friends.

Geoff had been part of this group
since they were all undergrads at
the University of London. They
seemed tight-knit, their conversations ranging seamlessly from
philosophical to deeply personal
topics. Eden had no problem keeping up with their witty banter, but
she balked at delving into more private topics. And from what she'd
seen so far, these guys really liked
to go deep.

Heather and Federico, the dark-
haired pair on the sofa, had been

dishing out the details of their latest couples' therapy session when Eden had escaped to the kitchen to fiddle with her tray of canapés. She couldn't understand why some people were willing to let all their personal stuff just hang out.

Geoff stood in the middle of the room and gestured toward the dining table. "I'm about ready to serve dinner. Care to move over here? Go ahead and bring your drinks with you."

The guests gathered around the tastefully decorated table, complete with ornately folded napkins and hand-lettered name cards for each place setting. Geoff hurried for-

ward and pulled Eden's chair back as she got to her seat.

"Thank you," she said. "Can I help you with anything more?"

He shook his head and squeezed her shoulder. "No, I'm on top of it. Just relax and get to know everyone." A fresh shard of guilt stabbed her as he smiled at her. The first chance she got, she needed to make it clear that he was in the friend zone. He disappeared into the kitchen.

Beverley, sitting to her right, touched Eden's hand. "It's great to finally meet you. Geoff can't stop talking about you. He tells us you work with his sister?"

Eden nodded, her rebellious stomach roiling even more. Did they think she and Geoff were dating? She arranged a polite smile on her face and replied to Beverley. "Yes, Ruby and I carry on the day-to-day management of the business, and Geoff is a silent partner."

Heather leaned forward. "Have you known Ruby long?"

"A couple of years. We met when we were both pitching a client for a video production job. Neither of us got hired, but we got along so well we thought we should join forces and go into business together."

Heather laughed. "What a story! And then Geoff invested in the business, too, right?"

Eden nodded. "Yes. I'm lucky to get on well with my business part-ners." She emphasized the words "business partners." Maybe it would send a clear signal that this was all Geoff was to her.

Beverley smiled as she leaned back in her chair. "You know, I al-ways find it interesting to learn how people got together. I made most of my closest friends back at univer-sity. I'm still in touch with a couple of people from elementary school, but the vast majority of them have fallen off by the wayside." She glanced at her husband. "Wouldn't you say so, Fred?"

Fred's head bobbed up and down in agreement. "It's exactly the same with me. Where did you say you grew up, Eden?"

"Surrey," Eden said. They looked at her, clearly expecting her to say more, but she didn't volunteer any further information. If she gave more details, they might realize who her family was, and that would lead to a bunch of questions she wasn't willing to answer. Not even Geoff knew her background, since she'd changed her name legally as soon as she'd turned eighteen. Eden Falconer, who had spent most of

her childhood as a fixture on reality TV shows along with the Falconer family, didn't exist anymore.

Right from Eden's conception, which was the climax of a TV series that followed her mother's IVF journey, her mother had welcomed cameras into the Falconers' lives to share their private moments. The breakdown of her parents' marriage had been splayed across the tabloids and TV screens, and when her mother had married Eden's stepfather, that, too, had been on an episode of Celebrity Weddings.

The cameras had been there to capture Eden's milestones as well. Nothing had been off-limits, not even the drama of Eden's first period or the day her mother had explained the birds and the bees. Eden had been desperate to escape that life. Now, at twenty-six, she was Eden *Tracey*, and she guarded her privacy as fiercely as her mother courted publicity.

The group chatted about childhood friendships and high school cliques and who was still in touch with whom. Eden let the conversation swirl around her. Maybe they'd move on to talk about something else.

No such luck. Heather turned toward her. "How about you, Eden?

Are you still friends with your BFF from high school?"

Eden injected a light tone in her voice. "No, I lost touch with my BFF. Hasn't everyone?" They all laughed and continued talking. Lost touch? More like she had ghosted him. These guys had better not ask any more questions about her background. Everything was a landmine she'd rather avoid.

Geoff came into the room balancing several plates on a large tray. "Ladies and gentlemen, dinner is served." Eden stood and helped him pass the plated-up entrées around the table. Geoff had made a vegetable tagine, served on a bed of couscous. The aromatic scents of ginger, garlic, cumin and cinnamon filled the air.

He took his place, basking for the next few minutes in his guests' compliments about how delicious the food was. His gaze kept drifting to Eden until she added her own compliments. He grinned as his shoulders relaxed. "Glad you like it."

Heather dabbed her mouth with a napkin. "Our marriage counselor was telling Federico and me that you can learn a lot about a person from the earliest memories they remember. It was really amazing! So, I thought it would be fun if we all

shared our first memories and tried to figure out what they say about us. Are you all game?"

Eager murmurs erupted around the table, but Eden's heart shrank. Beverley jumped in first, and the others followed one by one, talking about the earliest things they could remember from their childhood.

Eden eyed the kitchen door as the conversation got deeper and Geoff and his friends played armchair psychoanalyst and pulled apart each other's memories. Maybe she could grab some empty dishes and pretend to be clearing up. But Federico and Geoff were still eating.

As it came closer to her turn, she racked her brain for a red herring to deflect the question. She would not lie, of course, but why should she share her personal thoughts with this group of strangers? Even Geoff, whom she'd known for a couple of years, wasn't someone she wanted to delve into her past for. She didn't delve into her past for anyone.

Finally, it was her turn. Everyone's eyes turned to her. She twisted her napkin in her hands, her insides roiling. "I... I don't remember all that much from my childhood." *God, forgive me for that lie.* She cleared her throat. "Interesting to hear your stories, though.

Anyone need a top up to their drink?"

They were all silent for a couple of seconds. Beverley and Federico stared at her, while Heather dropped her gaze to her plate. Geoff stood. "Of course, where are my manners?" He went around filling up everyone's glasses.

A cell phone ring tone cut through the air, its bouncy melody jarring Eden's nerves. She jumped to her feet. "Sorry, I think that's mine." Why hadn't it rung five minutes earlier and saved her from having to be part of that conversation? She walked over to the armchair where she'd been sitting and pulled her phone out of her purse. She didn't recognize the number. "Hello?"

"Hi, Eden?" The voice was high, girlish. "This is Izzy, your sister."

Eden sat down. That was the last person she expected to hear from. "Izzy? Hi. What's up?"

"You said you live in Basildon, right?"

"Yes."

"I'm at the train station, but I don't remember your address. Could you... could you come and get me?"

Eden shook her head. This wasn't making sense. "You're here in Basildon?" She spoke louder than she intended, and the people at the dinner table turned to look at her. She lowered her voice. "Sure, I'll be there in about ten minutes. See you soon."

She slipped her phone back in her purse. What was Izzy doing here? She took a few steps toward the table. "I'm sorry, but something's come up and I have to leave. It's been great meeting all of you."

Geoff rushed to his feet. "You're going? You can't stay for dessert?"

"No, I need to leave now. Bye, everyone."

He followed her to the doorway. "Is something wrong? Aren't you feeling okay?"

Eden pulled her coat on and turned to face him. "My little sister just turned up at the train station and needs me to pick her up."

Geoff's face lit up. "Your sister? I didn't even know you had a sister. Why don't you bring her over? I'd love to meet her."

Absolutely not. Eden had no idea why Izzy was here, and the last thing she wanted to do was mix up her past and her present. She shook her head. "I'm not sure whether that's possible. It's getting late and your friends probably want to enjoy some grownup conversation. You don't want a teenager nobody knows hanging around."

"I really wouldn't mind, but I guess you know best. See you soon?" He leaned forward.

Eden moved her head so the kiss he'd intended for her cheek instead glanced off the top of her ear. "Thanks for tonight. Bye," she said, and hurried out to her Ford Fiesta, which she'd parked on Geoff's drive.

She brushed her fingers against her ear, where Geoff's attempted kiss had landed. *What is wrong with me?* Geoff was a nice guy, and he ticked all the important boxes: kind, hardworking, a Christian. Plus, he was easy on the eye, handsome in a dark-haired lupine sort of way. So, why was she throwing up walls?

No time to worry about that now. She needed to find out why Izzy was here.

Eden pulled her car up to Basildon train station. She spotted her sister immediately. Izzy stood at the pickup point behind the taxi rank, arms crossed tightly over her chest. Her collar was turned up against the sharp January wind that blew a tumble of brown curls across her face. The pink scarf around her neck was a bright splash of color against the drab gray brick of the station.

Izzy ran up to Eden's car and pulled open the passenger door, letting in a blast of freezing air. "Hi! That didn't take long." She shrugged off her backpack and slid onto the seat, then reached out and hugged Eden. "Thanks so much for coming."

Eden touched Izzy's cheek, her fingers brushing against the frames of her sister's glasses. "Your face is so cold! Good thing you didn't have to wait too long. Just put your bag in the back seat." Curiosity burned inside her, but she held back her questions. Izzy must have a reason for turning up like this.

"I hope I didn't pull you away from anything important," Izzy said.

Eden shook her head as she eased the car out onto the main road. Thanks to Izzy, she'd had the perfect excuse to leave Geoff's dinner party early. "No, nothing important. It's been ages! I haven't seen you since... my goodness, not since last summer when you were in London."

Eden had attended a ceremony at the Royal Society of Biology when Izzy received the Gold Certificate she won in the prestigious Biology Challenge. Their parents had been there, too, soaking up the reflected glory of Izzy's achievements. It was one of the infrequent times Eden saw her sister. Their ten-year age gap meant Izzy had been only eight when Eden left home. Even before Eden had gone, Izzy was living in a parallel and separate universe of Loom Bands and My Little Pony. They'd kept in touch more recently via social chat apps. Eden avoided going back to her hometown, and Izzy had never visited, let alone turned up unannounced like this.

"Did you have any trouble finding the way here on the train?"

"No, it was straightforward," Izzy said. "Took over two-and-a-half hours, though."

Eden navigated the roundabout and turned left onto Laindon Link. She glanced at Izzy as they waited for the traffic light to turn green. When did her kid sister grow up? She had clearly inherited their mother's deft hand with a makeup brush. Izzy was wearing only enough mascara and eyeliner to emphasize her striking brown eyes. Her complexion, a flawless tawny brown, was several shades fairer than Eden's, and free of the pimples that had plagued Eden when she'd been sixteen.

"Your hair looks amazing," Eden said. "Are you still going to Mum's guy, Julio?"

Izzy raised a hand to the dark brown curls which fell across her shoulders. "Aw, thanks. Julio's retired. Mum found this new stylist who's supposed to be a genius with curly hair."

"He's done a superb job," Eden said, moving the car forward as the lights went green. "How are you getting on with school? Do you like being in the sixth form?"

Izzy smiled. "The extra privileges are nice." They chatted for a while about Ridgeview School, the private school Eden had also attended.

Eden slowed her car to match the speed limit as they arrived at her neighborhood. "I guess you must be really busy if you have Oxford in your sights." She glanced at Izzy. "Didn't you mention Mum had arranged for you to be in a show about high schoolers trying to make it into Oxford?"

Izzy turned her head away. "I don't think I'll be doing that show anymore."

"Really? That's too bad, I guess. Wasn't Mum very excited about it?"

Izzy pushed her glasses up the bridge of her nose, mumbling a reply Eden didn't catch. Eden threw her a sidelong glance. Something was definitely off. When Eden had last seen her parents, her mother Elonora had been full of how Izzy

was going to be in a new reality TV show. The series was going to follow high school students as they tried for places at Britain's top universities. In addition to her Mensa-level IQ, Izzy studied hard, and it was obvious she was going to succeed on the path where Eden had failed. And she was going to do it all on TV, the surest route to their mother's approval.

Eden turned into the parking lot of her small apartment block, then settled her car in her dedicated spot. She turned to look at her sister. "Here we are."

Izzy followed her up the steps up to the second-floor apartment.

They stepped into the entryway and Izzy looked around her. "This is really nice."

Eden smiled, allowing herself a glow of pride about her apartment. It may have been a boxy and generic starter home in an anonymous housing estate, but it was all hers, earned by her own hard work. She'd livened up its default beige template, decorating with shades of gray, yellow, and blue. "Thank you. Let's go through to the living room."

Izzy stopped in the middle of the room and dropped her backpack on the floor. She crossed her arms tightly and stared at her feet.

Eden set her purse on the coffee table. "Can I get you a drink or something to eat?"

At the same moment Izzy blurted out, "I'm pregnant."

Eden blinked. "What?"

Izzy, her voice trembling, repeated her impossible words. "I'm pregnant."

It still made no sense to Eden. "Pregnant? With a baby? Are you sure?"

Izzy chewed her bottom lip and nodded. "I've taken three tests. They're all positive."

A dozen questions crowded Eden's mind, fighting for which would come out first. Who was the father? How far along? Since when had Izzy been doing... that? What do Mum and Dad think? But before she had a chance to ask any of them, she caught the look on Izzy's face. Those questions would have to wait. She stepped forward and wrapped her arms around her sister. Izzy leaned against Eden, her slight body shaking as she sobbed quietly.

Eden stroked her hair. Izzy was just a kid herself. How could she be having a baby? She must be terrified. No wonder she had shown up unannounced. This wasn't the sort of news you dropped in a text message. When Izzy's sobs subsided,

Eden pulled her gently toward the sofa and handed her a box of tissues.

Izzy grabbed one and blew her nose. She took a shaky breath. "I found out a couple of days ago. I didn't want to believe it, and that's why I took all those tests. Kieran and I had never—it only happened once." She ducked her head.

Eden grabbed at the name. "Kieran. Is that the—is he the—"

Izzy nodded. "He's my boyfriend. I told him this morning."

"And what does he say?"

"Not much. He's as shocked as I am."

"And have you told Mum and Dad?"

"Not yet. They're going to kill me!" Izzy's eyes filled up again. "I don't know what to do."

Eden put an arm around her. Izzy was probably right: their mother was going to hit the roof. But saying that wouldn't help. She struggled to find more encouraging words. "We'll figure it out, sweetheart. It's an enormous shock and I don't have any immediate answers, but we'll work it out. You're not in this alone, okay?"

Izzy blew her nose again. "Thank you."

They sat quietly as Eden's mind buzzed. They needed to get Izzy to a doctor and have her checked out. What about school? How would all this affect Izzy's plans for her education and career? And what about this Kieran character? What sort of boy was he? Was he going to vanish off into the ether? And their parents. Eden shuddered. Their mother Elonora, who saw her children's success as an extension of her own, would not take this news well. No wonder Izzy had come to her, the sister she barely saw.

"Does Mum know you're here?" Eden asked.

Izzy stiffened. "No."

"Okay, the first thing we'll do is tell her you're here and you'll be spending the night. You will stay here tonight, won't you?"

Izzy nodded. "Yes, please."

"Okay, great. I'll leave her a message and then I'll take you down to Hatbrook tomorrow." The least she could do was be with Izzy when they told their parents. Eden was used to disappointing Elonora. She could absorb the initial heat of her mother's reaction.

Izzy threw her arms around Eden. "I'm so glad I came here! Thanks so much."

Eden hugged her back, warmth rising in her heart. "I'm glad you

came, too." She prayed silently. *Lord, thank you for encouraging Izzy to come here. But what are we going to do?*

Chapter Two

NOAH CHAPLIN wheeled the last pile of stacked chairs into the storage room at Grace Community Church. His mind still buzzed from the energy of tonight's youth group meeting.

They'd been studying Psalm 37, and those teens weren't afraid to ask some tough questions. Why did God allow terrible things to happen to good people? Was there any point trying to live a righteous life

when the bad guys seem to come out ahead? That's exactly what he was here for: to pastor and teach these young people as they grew in their faith and grappled with applying it in their lives.

He'd skimmed over verse 34: "Delight thyself also in the Lord: and he shall give thee the desires of thine heart." That was a verse he always struggled with. He did his best to serve God, but this wasn't exactly the life he'd envisioned for himself at twenty-seven. Well, the pastoring was, and getting to work with this amazing bunch of kids was exactly what he was meant to do. But after the bustle and buzz of his youth ministry was over, the desires of his heart did not include him going home to a dark, empty apartment.

True, he sometimes hung out with his friends, and tonight he'd be having dinner with his parents. But in between those highlights, there were far too many of the other kind of evening. The more common kind, punctuated by microwave meals for one and a silence so heavy he'd sometimes turn on the TV just to have any kind of noise and create the illusion of company.

He slid the stack of chairs into place and closed the storage room door. How many chairs had he put

away over the years? Must be half a million at least, growing up as a pastor's kid and now as a youth pastor. Setting stuff up for meetings and putting it all away again was one of the many time-consuming chores that came with the territory. But there was a lot to be thankful for. God was using him here, and he cared deeply for all the young people who came to Grace Community.

Noah glanced up at a teenage boy who now shoved a table to the side of the room. There was never a shortage of volunteers to put things away after youth group, and Kieran Haynes was one of the most helpful. Come to think of it, Kieran seemed a lot more keen than usual. The other young people had left, but even after all the clear-up work was done, the boy lingered in the vestibule, hand churning in his bushy brown hair.

Kieran turned toward the door, then spun around again. "Pastor Noah? Do you have a moment?"

Noah was expected to dinner at his parents' house in a few minutes, but a tug in his spirit told him he needed to postpone his visit. "Yes, no problem. Do you want to go over to my office? I'll just lock up here first and see you in a minute."

Kieran nodded and shuffled down the hallway toward the

church offices. Noah secured the storage room door and pulled out his cell phone to text his dad. Thomas Chaplin was senior pastor at Grace Community Church. He'd understand why Noah was going to be late.

Kieran stood outside the office door, hands stuffed in his pockets, shifting his weight from foot to foot.

"Come in," Noah said. He walked behind his desk in the small, crowded office and sat down, resting his elbows on the table.

Kieran sat opposite him. Although the boy had asked for the meeting, he seemed unwilling to speak now that he was here. He kneaded his hands together, then rubbed the back of his neck.

Noah gave him a gentle prompt. "Everything okay at school?"

"Yeah, school's fine."

"And your uncle, how's he doing?" Kieran had moved in with his uncle at twelve, when he'd lost his mother.

"Uncle Tim's okay." Kieran drew a deep breath and let it out slowly. "Pastor Noah? I--" he looked down at his lap and pushed his hands through his hair.

Kieran's face contorted, mouth working, but no words came out. Noah's heart rate ticked up, and he

sent up a silent prayer for wisdom. Whatever was on the boy's mind, it must be huge. Best not to rush him.

"Do you think God can forgive me?" Kieran's voice was strangled, his eyes moist, as he turned to Noah.

Oh dear. What had the boy done? Aloud, Noah said, "Of course, God can forgive you as long as you ask Him. Are you all right?"

"Yeah, I'm fine. It's just that I've made a big mistake. I did something I know I wasn't supposed to do." Once he began to speak, his words spilled out. "You tell us all the time about how God has made marriage special and how we're supposed to

54

wait and try to flee temptation. But I wasn't able to do that. My girl-friend... it was my fault. I sort of talked her into it. We started fool-ing around and we went a lot fur-ther than I thought we would and... She told me today that she's pregnant."

Noah sucked in a deep breath. Oh no. How on earth...? Kieran was something of a heartthrob at Grace Community, and several of the young girls in church followed him around with doe eyes, but Noah had detected nothing special between Kieran and any of them. He hadn't even known Kieran had a girlfriend.

The boy was one of the most active members of the youth group, in church whenever the doors opened. Ever since he'd become a Christian three years ago, Kieran had been like a sponge, soaking up whatever spiritual teaching he could get. He was the last boy Noah would have expected to land in this kind of trouble.

Noah let his breath out slowly. "Okay. Is she all right? Has she told her parents?"

"She's scared and upset. She said I was the first person she's told. It's all my fault because I couldn't..." Kieran took a shaky breath. He pushed his hands into his hair. "I got us into this, and I said I'll stand by her. I love her. But I have no idea what we're going to do. And I feel so bad that I've let God down." His voice hitched, and he buried his face in his hands.

Noah held up his hand. "Hold on a minute before we go any further. God loves you and I can tell that you love Him. God has a plan where sex has a defined place. But He knows it's hard to stick to that plan, and He completely understands our weaknesses. He's ready to forgive us when we fall short.

"Remember King David? He was an adulterer and a murderer. We all mess up. But as long as you or I con-

fess our sins to him, he is faithful and just and will forgive us and help us make things right. Okay?"

Kieran passed a hand over his eyes. His voice was husky when he replied. "Okay."

Noah watched as Kieran wiped away another tear. When news of this got out, Kieran was going to face a lot of judgement and finger-pointing, some of it coming from members of his own church. But he would not be the sort of pastor who made people feel they were worse sinners than everybody else, just because their particular sin had vis-ible consequences. Kieran needed grace, and so did this girl, whoever she was.

He touched Kieran's arm. "God can and does forgive our sins when we ask. Above all else, He loves you and wants to be close to you. We'll take a moment and pray about that, but we also need to figure out what's going to happen now. There's a baby coming who will need a loving and safe home, and a young lady who needs a lot of support and help."

Kieran nodded, wiping his eyes with his sleeve. "I want to do everything I can. She's so amazing."

"Have I met her before? Does she come to Grace Community?"

"No. She goes to St. Matthews. She's a Christian, too." He pulled his phone out of his pocket. The screen lit up, and he scrolled through some pictures before handing his phone to Noah. "Her name is Izzy. Well, it's really Isolde, but she said everyone except her mother calls her Izzy."

Noah's heart jolted as he looked at the photo of the smiling, pretty girl. It couldn't be. The dark eyes behind rectangular-framed glasses, flawless brown skin, shoulder-length curly hair... She looked exactly like another teenage girl he'd once known years ago when he was a teenager himself.

Even her expression tugged at his memory. In the picture, she looked as though she'd heard something funny and had suppressed her laughter until it finally exploded out at the moment the camera captured her image.

Noah found his voice. "What's her surname?"

"Falconer."

Noah closed his eyes and nodded. Of course. This had to be the little sister Eden had sometimes talked about. He looked at Kieran. "Her mum is Elonora Falconer." It wasn't a question.

Kieran nodded. "Yeah, from that TV show. But Izzy is nothing like her. She's really sweet."

"How did you meet?" Noah asked. He needed to concentrate on what Kieran was saying, not lose himself in thoughts about the girl who'd been his best friend until she'd disappeared from town and ghosted him eight years ago. He stared at the phone. Where was Eden? Did she know she was going to be an aunt? Why did she just vanish? *Stop. Focus on Kieran.* He wrenched his gaze away from the picture and slid the phone back to Kieran.

"She was on her school debating team and they came over to my school for a debating contest. We sat together at lunch and just got talking and found we had a lot in common. I asked her out, and we started dating." Kieran gazed at the picture on his phone, brushing it with his fingers. "I won't let her down."

Noah glanced at Kieran's face, which still had traces of his pre-adolescent chubbiness around his cheeks. Noah had watched this kid grow up in Grace Community. He was still so young. This was going to test Kieran's character like nothing else he'd ever been through. "I'm glad you feel that way. There's going to be a lot to think about and figure out. For one thing, her parents are probably going to have a lot to say. But I'm here for you, okay?"

Kieran nodded. "Thank you."

"Have you talked to your uncle?"

Kieran looked up. "Not yet. He's out of town again. I'll tell him, but I want to see Izzy first. She was afraid of telling her mum, so she said she was going to talk to her sister first. Her sister lives in Basildon, so she went up there."

Basildon. So, that's where Eden had disappeared to. No, stop thinking about Eden. Focus. This was about Kieran and Izzy, not about him and his former best friend. He looked up at Kieran. "Shall we take a moment to pray?"

"I'd like that." Kieran bowed his head as Noah talked to God, asking Him for wisdom and grace, to watch over the baby and mother-to-be, and to show them all what they needed to do.

When he was done, Kieran looked up, wiping his eyes with the corner of his sleeve. "Thanks, Pastor Noah. I feel a lot better."

"I'm glad. And thanks for coming to me. I'm always here if you need me. I mean that." Noah smiled, but his experience and everything he'd ever studied told him Kieran was

up against massive odds. Orphaned at twelve, father-to-be at seventeen. On paper, it was a statistical nightmare. And in his time as a pastor, Noah had never had to deal with an issue of this magnitude. Did he even have the wisdom to give Kieran the support he would need? *Lord, we need you. Please help us.*

Chapter Three

ELL BEFORE seven o'clock the next morning, Eden sat at her kitchen table, her fingers curled around a mug of green tea. Her gaze fell on Izzy's backpack, sitting in the corner of the room. No, it hadn't been a dream. Her sixteen-year-old sister was here, pregnant. It was even more unbelievable because Izzy had never set a foot wrong in her life. She was the apple of her mother's eye and never

seemed to have any trouble meeting Elonora's expectations. And Elonora had huge dreams for her second child.

For a while, when Eden had been trying to get her career started, she'd resented hearing about all Izzy's successes, as her little sister blew past all the regular milestones and quickly proved she was exponentially more gifted. Elonora never failed to trumpet every last one of Izzy's triumphs to the world. Besides being a brilliant scholar, Izzy excelled at everything she tried: piano, tennis, art, golf–her abilities seemed boundless. She'd even been nominated to give a speech in the British Parliament when a select committee had been discussing possible new laws for fee-paying schools.

But as Eden had gotten older and started exchanging text messages directly with Izzy, she soon learned that, far from being a stuck-up know-it-all, her little sister was sweet and unpretentious, never taking her brains or talents for granted. And now Izzy had reached out to her, had trusted her, despite their not being close. She would do her utmost to prove she was worthy of that trust.

Izzy padded into the kitchen wearing one of Eden's nightshirts.

The purple cotton shirt was a couple of sizes too big for her, swamping her slight frame. With her sleep tousled hair and make-up free face, she looked closer to twelve than sixteen. She rubbed her eyes under her glasses. "Morning."

Eden smiled. "Hey. Did you sleep all right?"

"I did, actually. Better than I have in a long while." Izzy pulled up a chair and sat at the table.

"Can I get you some breakfast?"

Izzy wrinkled her nose and shook her head. "I don't know. I'm feeling a bit queasy."

"Morning sickness, huh? I remember reading somewhere that crackers or rice cakes can help."

"Okay, crackers then, please." As Eden stood up and went to the cupboard Izzy added, "With peanut butter, please."

Eden arranged the crackers on a plate, spreading a thin layer of peanut butter on each of them. She slid the plate over to Izzy, then settled back at her place and sipped her tea. "Are we going to tell Mum and Dad today?"

Izzy's shoulders slumped. She nodded slowly. "I guess I shouldn't put it off any longer."

"Do you know how far along you are?"

Izzy chewed her bottom lip. "I know the date when we... when it happened." She looked down at her hands. "I know I messed up. I'm supposed to be a Christian."

"Hey, stop that." Eden reached for Izzy's hand. "Don't beat yourself up. Sometimes Christians have this idea that sex outside of marriage is the worst kind of unforgivable crime ever. Yes, it is a sin. But just like lying or stealing or anything else, God forgives us when we come back to Him."

Eden paused. She knew all about utterly failing as a Christian. Should she tell Izzy? It might encourage her sister not to feel so bad. A warm tear dropped onto her hand. Eden swallowed hard, the words sticking in her throat. No, she couldn't tell Izzy about... that. She couldn't tell anyone.

She squeezed Izzy's hand. "Christians mess up, too. All the time. But we keep trying."

Izzy sniffed and grabbed a fresh tissue. "Thanks. I wish I could be like you. You're so strong in your faith."

Eden flinched. She might be firmer in her faith now, but it hadn't always been that way.

Izzy sat up and tucked a strand of hair behind her ear. "What were you saying about how far along I am?"

Eden picked up her phone. "I found this pregnancy due date calculator online. It can tell us when the baby's coming. Just a guesstimate, of course, until you see a doctor. Do you remember when you had your last period?"

Izzy's brow furrowed. "Um... it wasn't last month. I think it was on November 1st."

Eden entered the information into the calculator. "And how many days is your cycle?" Boy, was it weird to ask Izzy such questions.

They'd never talked about anything more personal than their taste in nail art, and here she was probing deep into Izzy's business.

"Thirty days, I think," Izzy said.

"Okay." Eden typed quickly and watched the screen change. She gave Izzy the phone. "You're about nine weeks pregnant, and the baby's due in the summer. It might even come around the same time as your birthday."

Izzy stared at the phone, then looked up at Eden. "How can I be nine weeks pregnant? It hasn't been that long since Kieran and I went all the way."

"Apparently, they count the date from your last period. I don't understand why, but that's just how they do it. So you're about two months along."

"Two months," Izzy repeated. "And it lasts nine months."

Eden nodded. Just over half a year until the baby was here. "I'm going to be an aunt."

Izzy smiled. "Yeah." Her smile faded. "If Mum doesn't kill me first."

Eden stroked Izzy's hand. She didn't blame her sister for fixating on their mother's reaction. Their father—rather, Eden's stepdad and Izzy's biological father—would be surprised and shocked, of course, but Elonora was the more volatile one. She kept everyone walking on eggshells.

"She might take the news better than we think," Eden said, injecting a heavy dose of confidence into her voice. "I'll come with you, of course. We can tell her together."

Izzy's eyes widened. She grabbed Eden's hand. "Thank you! It'll be so good to have you there."

Eden squeezed Izzy's hand. She hadn't been in Hatbrook in years, apart from one quick visit to attend her grandmother's funeral. But she wasn't about to let Izzy face their mother alone with this life-altering

news. She finished the last of her tea. "We don't have to go straight away, though. Maybe we can stop by the mall first, do a bit of shopping before we go."

Izzy grinned. "Sounds great." She moistened her index finger with her tongue and dabbed up the remaining crumbs on her plate, then stuck her finger in her mouth.

Eden smiled. Izzy had done that thing with the crumbs right from when she was a toddler. It had been too long since they'd spent time together. She'd been so occupied with staying away from Hatbrook that she'd let her sister become a virtual stranger. But maybe she could fix that.

Izzy stood. "I'll just grab a shower before we go."

Eden's phone buzzed as Izzy left. She checked the screen. Geoff wanted to know how Eden's sister was and hoped the surprise visit was going well. Why did he have to be so nice? He tried so hard, always checking on her, reaching out and trying to get closer. But even a simple question like this set her on edge and made her want to raise up her shields.

Telling him why Izzy was here would lead to more questions about her family. Geoff was a decent guy,

fun to hang out with as long as she could keep him at arm's length. But there was no way she was going to pull away all the layers and let him see inside her, to glimpse the tangled bundle of issues from her family and her past.

It would be just like those horrible nightmares of being naked in front of a bunch of strangers, exposed to their judgement, shock, and pity.

She typed a reply. *She's fine, thanks for asking. Hope you have a good weekend.*

Half an hour later, a freshly showered Izzy came back into the living room, phone in hand. "Do you mind if we meet Kieran before we go home? He said his pastor gave him some brochures and stuff about Christian ministries that can help us. He'll be at church. And I want to see him before talking to Mum."

Eden nodded. "Okay, not a problem. Tell me about Kieran. How long have you been dating?"

Izzy's face brightened. "About a year."

"How old is he?"

"Seventeen."

So, he was a kid just like Izzy. Two babies having a baby. "And what's he doing? I assume he's in school?"

"Yes, he's in his final year at Hat-brook Comprehensive School."

"What's his family like?"

"He lost both his parents when he was young, so he lives with his uncle. It's just the two of them. His uncle's a petroleum engineer and he's away a lot."

Eden frowned. So, this young man was left to his own devices for large chunks of time. That was a recipe for trouble. "And you said he's involved with the church."

"Yes, he's a leader in the youth group there."

At least that was a point in the boy's favor. Being active in church meant he had some good influences in his life and hopefully wasn't into less wholesome pursuits. Although, of course, that didn't mean he wouldn't be immune from getting into trouble, as the present situation showed. "I'd love to meet him."

Izzy smiled. "I think you'd like him. He's my best friend."

Eden's heart squeezed. She'd had a best friend, too, when she was a teen, a boy who was also active in the youth group at church. And, like Izzy, she'd also fallen in love with him. Perhaps it was for the best that he hadn't felt the same way about her. Otherwise, who knew where things could have

gone? She might have been in a similar situation to Izzy.

Or she might have been happily married to him by now. But this wasn't the time to think about the unrealistic daydreams she'd once harbored about Noah Chaplin. A future with Noah had never been an option. He'd chosen someone else, and they were probably married with 2.5 children.

That ship had sailed, and it was pointless to think about might-have-beens. She stood and picked up her purse. "Let's get going. We can stop at the bookstore and grab some books and just treat ourselves before I drive you down to Hatbrook."

Izzy grinned. "Okay."

Eden steered her car onto the motorway offramp leading toward Hatbrook village. "We're nearly there."

She and Izzy had spent the morning at the mall shopping, splurging on a manicure, and sharing brunch at a café. A perfect bonding session. Pity it took a major life crisis for her to spend quality time with her sister.

She liked the young woman she was getting to know. No matter what happened, she was going to make more of an effort to be a part of Izzy's life from now on.

They'd had a pleasant chat for most of the one-hour drive south from Basildon, but they had spent the last several minutes of their trip in silence. Izzy's voice suddenly broke through the muffled hum of the traffic speeding outside around them. "If Mum kicks me out, can I come live with you?"

Eden glanced at her. The joking remark she was about to make withered on her lips when she registered her sister's face. Izzy's eyes were large, her lips trembling. She clearly wasn't trying to be funny.

Eden touched her arm. "Mum won't kick you out. But of course you can stay with me. You're welcome at any time. I mean that."

"Thank you." They drove on for a few more minutes. Izzy said, "Shouldn't you have taken the right turn off that roundabout?"

"No, this is the right way. We're going to St. Matthew's Church, aren't we?"

"St. Matthews? No. We're meeting Kieran at Grace Community Church. That's where he goes."

Eden shot her sister a sharp glance. Grace Community Church? She had assumed that Kieran and Izzy went to the same church.

Grace Community had been Eden's church when she was a teenager. The church where she had given her life to the Lord. The church where Noah's father was senior pastor.

"I didn't realize that," she said. "I'll just use this petrol station to turn around." She maneuvered the car in the right direction and in a few more minutes she pulled up into the parking lot of Grace Community Church, Hatbrook.

It had been almost eight years since she'd last been here. It had changed, gotten bigger. They'd finished building the annex they'd been fundraising for. The church members must have come through. This place had once been the center of her life. It had witnessed so many milestones. Her becoming a Christian, her first love, her first heartbreak.

Izzy gripped the car door handle. "I'll try not to be long. I just need to see Kieran and pick up some things he said his pastor wants to pass on to us."

Eden watched her go up the path and into the church building. Hopefully, Izzy was right about not staying too long. She really needed the bathroom, but could wait until they got home.

Eden looked around the parking lot. It was about one third full. Saturday afternoon. That would be the senior ladies' fellowship. Judging from the number of cars, attendance was decent. Apart from the new annex, the one-story church building looked just as she remembered it. She had spent hours upon hours here back when she was a teenager.

Grace Community had been a place of refuge from the craziness of her home life. No one here had seemed bothered about who she was or, more importantly, who her family was. Either they didn't follow reality TV shows or the tabloid press, or they were too polite to bring it up with her.

A few more minutes ticked by and Izzy still hadn't returned. Eden shifted in her seat. She really needed the bathroom. Maybe she could just hurry into the church, use the facilities, and hurry out again.

She stepped out of the car and walked toward the front door. The sun was setting, making the leafless branches on the Japanese maple trees stand out in stark relief. There was a sharp bite in the air.

Eden pushed the heavy church doors hard as she stepped into the vestibule. It had new flooring now.

They had replaced the ratty old green runner carpet with plush wall-to-wall royal blue carpets. It looked good.

Directly in front of her, the centerpiece of the space, was a large mural with Jesus in the center and people of all ages and ethnicities walking up to him, some of them dragging huge loads. Underneath it all in beautifully lettered text were the words from Matthew 11:28: "Come unto me all ye that labor and are heavy laden, and I will give you rest."

She stood staring at the mural for a moment before heading left down the hallway to the ladies' restroom.

A short while later she came back out. She rounded the corner and froze, as though she'd rammed into an electrified fence.

Izzy was coming from across the vestibule, holding hands with a handsome teenage boy. Walking next to them was Noah Chaplin. He was taller than she remembered, his shoulders broader, his body filled out in all the right places from the scrawny frame she remembered. His thick dark hair was slightly rumpled, as though he still had the habit of running a hand through it when he was thinking. His eyes met hers and he stopped in his tracks.

Eden stared at him, tongue-tied, the sound of blood rushing through her ears.

Noah recovered first, and he stepped forward, hand stretched out. "Eden. Good to see you." He gripped her hand.

"Hi." Her voice sounded like it was coming from miles away. "Good to see you, too."

Izzy looked from one to the other. "You know each other?"

"Yes." Eden forced herself to look into Noah's hazel eyes. "How's your wife doing?"

He frowned. "My wife? I'm not married."

A rush of heat seared Eden's face. "Not married? I thought that—" she stared at him, her words drying up. When she'd left Hatbrook, he'd been engaged to Angela, the gorgeous daughter of the new associate pastor.

Noah dropped her hand. "We didn't get married." He gestured toward Kieran. "I understand you haven't met Kieran. Kieran Haynes, this is Eden, Izzy's sister."

Kieran held out his hand. "You're Eden? Wow, glad to meet you."

Eden barely registered Kieran's presence. Noah wasn't married? What had happened? She must look like an idiot standing here gaping.

Kieran was still holding out his hand. She took it. "Nice to meet you, too. Um, Izzy, we'd better be off." She spoke in the general direction of the two men. "Nice seeing you. Bye."

Turning around, she rushed toward the door. The cold air blasted her hot cheeks as she stepped outside and made a beeline for her car. She wasn't supposed to run into Noah. This was meant to be a quick bathroom break, not her running headlong into the guy she'd been trying to avoid for the past eight years. What was his role with Kieran and Izzy? She pushed the button on the key fob and the lights on her car responded. She pulled open the door and sat in the driver's seat, resting her elbows on the dashboard and her forehead in her hands. Noah. After all these years.

The passenger door opened and Izzy slid into her seat. She stared wide-eyed at Eden, her face one big question mark. "I didn't know you knew Pastor Noah. And why did you think he was married?"

Chapter Four

"UM, WHAT?" Eden said. Izzy's question had been perfectly audible. She was just stalling for time, trying to avoid giving a direct answer.

"I said, why did you think Pastor Noah was married?"

Eden shrugged. "I knew him a while ago and the last I heard, he was engaged and was completely wrapped up with his fiancée."

Izzy tugged at her seatbelt and clicked it in place. "Oh. Well, that must have been quite a while ago. As far as I know, Pastor Noah has always been single. Kieran says a lot of church ladies would rather like to become Mrs. Noah Chaplin."

Eden clenched her teeth. "Really?"

"Yeah. Kieran said it gets quite embarrassing sometimes. I'd never met him before today, but seeing him now, I get why they'd be after him. He's pretty good-looking for an older guy."

Eden laughed. "Older guy? Wow, thanks for that. I feel ancient now! He's my age, you know."

"Is he? Sorry, I didn't mean it badly. He looks, like, thirty or something."

Eden started the engine. "He's twenty-seven, pretty much the same as me. What did he give you? What are those?"

Izzy held up a handful of pamphlets and brochures. "He gave us some information about the local crisis pregnancy center and a few other ministries and places he thought might be useful. I'm glad Kieran told him, and I think Pastor Noah is just as great as Kieran says he is. I could tell he really cares. He wasn't all judgy or anything."

So, Noah was Kieran's pastor and knew about the baby. Eden steered the car down the road, turning left at a T-junction.

Izzy was still talking. "You know, I might start going to Grace Community instead. I haven't been feeling comfortable at St. Matthews for a while. I can't imagine telling Pastor Forbes about having a baby and all this."

Eden mumbled a response. Noah as Izzy's counselor? Part of her recoiled at the thought. She had ghosted him, walking out of his life with no explanation. If the awkwardness of today's meeting was any sign of the future, every run-in

with him was going to be excruciat-
ingly embarrassing.

She stopped at a pedestrian cross-
ing and glanced at Izzy. Her sister
sat clutching the brochures Noah
had given her. Eden sighed and
pushed on the gas pedal. She
needed to stop making this all about
her. If Noah hadn't changed, he was
probably a great youth pastor. He'd
provide her sister and Kieran with
solid counsel and support. She
needed to get over herself. It wasn't
as though she had to see him or talk
to him, anyway.

She drove down the old High
Street, taking in the familiar sights.
The library on the right and on the

left, the ancient 13th century stone church that was the focal point of the street. Several of the shops had changed. A few fashion boutiques remained, plus a new fast-food restaurant and the hair salon.

They came to a quiet oak tree-lined street and Eden stopped in front of a tall wrought-iron gate. They were here. She rolled down her window and leaned her elbow onto the open windowsill, making sure her face was visible to the security camera on the gate. A buzzer sounded, and the gate slid open.

Eden drove on to the stone-paved driveway. Her mother's red Jaguar was there, as was her father's black

BMW. Good, it seemed they were both home. It would be better to break the news to both of them. She pulled the car to a stop and turned toward Izzy. Izzy stared straight ahead, her breath quickening. Eden reached out for her hand. "Shall we pray before going in?"

Izzy nodded, clutching at Eden's fingers.

Eden paused for a moment, gathering her thoughts and turning her focus to the God she knew cared even for the sparrows. "Lord, we ask for your wisdom as we speak to Mum and Dad now. We ask that your grace would surround us and that you would help them receive this news with peace and calm. We ask that all of us would be what Izzy needs right now. Help us know you are with us and that you will go before us. We thank you because you have never forsaken us, and your love always surrounds us. In Jesus' name. Amen."

Izzy squeezed her hand. "Amen."

Eden looked at her sister and drew a deep breath. "Let's go in."

5

Chapter Five

NOAH STOOD in the church lobby, his heart still racing. Eden had actually been here, in the flesh. He stared at the blank space where she had been standing a minute ago. She had stood there and looked at him, acting as though they'd seen each other last week.

Why would she do that? What had he ever done to her to make her ghost him like she had?

Out of the blue, his phone calls to her had started going to a recorded message saying her number was no longer in service. He'd tried to track her down on social media, but she had vanished from there, too. Her profile no longer existed.

And the one time he'd plucked up the courage to go to her home, he couldn't even get past the front gate. Someone, talking through a speaker in the security system, had told him that Eden had gone to university. They wouldn't tell him where.

Then Angela had dumped him. Noah could have used a friend back then, the kind of friend Eden had always been, until she suddenly wasn't. And now she had just turned up. He wanted answers.

"Pastor Noah?"

Noah whirled around. Kieran was watching him. How long had the boy been talking?

Kieran held up the brochures Noah had given him. "Thanks again for all this information. I'll be off now."

Noah shook his head to clear the fog. "All right, Kieran. It was great to see you and to meet Izzy as well. She's a lovely girl."

Kieran grinned. "Yeah, she is. Her sister seems nice, too."

"Um, yeah. I'll speak to you soon." Kieran strolled away, and Noah stared at the ground, rubbing the back of his neck.

Noah's dad Thomas, senior pastor of Grace Community, came up to him. "Did I just see your friend leaving the building? What was her name again? Oh yes, Eden. Was she in here?"

"Yes."

"There's a face I haven't seen in ages. Did she come to meet you?"

Noah shook his head. "No, she was here with her sister. There's a bit of trouble there." He explained the situation to his father, giving a

quick summary of what was going on between Izzy and Kieran.

Thomas listened quietly, stroking his chin. "That's a tough one. Both of them under eighteen, eh? I'm glad they came to you."

Noah nodded. "I'm grateful Kieran approached me, but I'm not sure I'm equipped to handle it." Given his track record of failed relationships, what wisdom did he have to offer these young people?

He could tell them all about dumping and being dumped. He had intimate knowledge of how to survive a breakup, but not how to grow in maturity and build a bond that would last. With a baby on the way, Kieran and Izzy needed solid support from someone who was not a loser in the relationship department.

Noah looked at his father. "Maybe I should pass this one on to you since you're the senior pastor. It's above my head, to be honest."

Thomas patted his shoulder. "No way. It's not above your head. I have every confidence that you can help them. If you need to consult me about anything, I'm here for you, of course. But since you've already built a rapport and trust with them, it's best that you continue to be their contact point."

Noah opened his mouth, but Thomas turned toward the door before he could speak. "We'll talk about this later. Right now, we have to get moving. You know how your mother hates being kept waiting when she's got a meal on."

Noah smiled. He understood. His mother Rachel was a stickler for timekeeping, and few things annoyed her as much as when people showed up late for dinner. He followed his father out of the building and they walked across the parking lot to the Parsonage that was nestled on a quiet cul-de-sac behind the church.

Thomas fished his keys out of his pocket and let them inside. "Rachel, were home."

Noah's mother's voice floated into the hallway from the kitchen. "I'm about ready to plate up. Just go wash up and get yourselves to the table."

The unmistakable scents of a roast dinner saturated the air. Noah's stomach rumbled in anticipation. Rachel had made his favorite meal.

"I'll use the upstairs bathroom," Thomas said. He pointed a thumb to the washroom just down the hallway. "You go ahead and use that one."

As Noah headed to the bathroom, he glimpsed his father's study through a door to the right. Books and papers jumbled in a higgledy-piggledy fashion over the table and spilled out of the bookshelves. A layer of dust coated the flat surfaces, and the carpet looked like it hadn't seen a vacuum cleaner in a while. Noah frowned. Tidiness wasn't his father's strongest quality. But ordinarily, his mother would have made this room conform to the rest of the house, which she kept impeccably clean. Why was this one room in such a state?

Noah washed his hands and headed to the dining room. His

mother walked in carrying a carved pork roast. She set it on the middle of the table, and he bent forward to kiss her cheek. She hugged him, oven mitts still on her hands. Her familiar scent of Yardley's Roses perfume mingled with the savory aroma of the food.

"I wasn't expecting a roast dinner. You've pulled out all the stops."

She smiled and patted his back. "I'll be going out of town on a business trip early tomorrow, so you get your Sunday dinner a day early." She headed back into the kitchen.

Noah took his place at the table and glanced at his father. Thomas's gaze was fixed on his plate, his expression blank. That would be the third Sunday this month Rachel was traveling on business. His mother wasn't involved much with the church anymore since her freelance executive training business took up a lot of her time, but she'd always been in the front pew on Sunday morning.

She came back with a platter of roast potatoes and Yorkshire pudding. When they were all seated around the table, Thomas held out his hands and the family joined in the familiar circle they'd made countless mealtimes before. "Thank you, Lord, for this meal and for the hands that made it. We ask that you bless it for our nourishment and health. Amen."

"Help yourself." Rachel gestured at the food.

Noah didn't need a second invitation. He took a couple of slices of meat, a few potatoes, and Yorkshire pudding, and drizzled gravy over everything. He looked up at his mother. "Where's your trip to this time?"

"I'll be training some C suite executives up in Leeds on how to achieve leadership excellence. It'll be a three-day session."

Noah sliced into a potato. "Strange that they're doing their training on a Sunday."

"Oh, they're not starting on Sunday. The training begins on Tuesday."

Tuesday? So, she didn't have to leave tomorrow unless she wanted to.

"May I have some gravy, please?" Thomas was looking at his wife.

"I wanted to take advantage of being in Leeds to network with some business contacts," Rachel said, talking over Thomas. "Nothing beats meeting face to face. I've got appointments lined up all through Monday."

"May I have the gravy, please?" Thomas spoke slightly louder, but

Rachel continued talking, as though oblivious to what he had said.

Noah reached over for the gravy boat, which was on the other side of his mother's plate. He passed it over to his father.

Thomas grasped the handle. "Thank you."

Finally, Rachel turned her head and looked at Thomas. "Oh, did you want that?"

Noah stared at her. Under the innocuous words he detected a hard, brittle edge. Thomas didn't reply but poured the gravy onto his food.

What was going on with these two? Noah put another bite of food into his mouth, chewing in silence.

The dish was one of his favorites, but right now, it tasted like sandpaper.

Chapter Six

EDEN'S STOMACH rolled as she and Izzy walked up to the front door of the Falconer family home. Her gaze swept across the front of the house. The mid-18th century brick and flint farmhouse had been extensively expanded on a home makeover show when she was twelve.

The TV crew had spent ages shooting and re-shooting the "big reveal," the moment the Falconers were supposedly seeing their madeover home for the first time. A memory of the show's producer's voice came back to Eden. "Let's try it again. I need more energy from you, Eden. Make sure to really gasp. Put your hands over your mouth. Maybe jump around a bit, okay? Elonora, you were great. Let's keep it exactly the same. Everyone ready? Once more from the top."

Eden put her hand on the door handle. What would her mother's reaction to Izzy's pregnancy be when there were no cameras rolling? They walked into the front hallway. Piano music came from the lounge, one of Beethoven's sonatas.

That meant their father Gregory was home.

When they walked into the lounge, he jumped up from the piano stool and came over to them, arms outstretched. "Girls! Hello!" He hugged each of them in turn. He looked at Eden. "It's so good to see you again. It's been a while since you were here, hasn't it?"

Eden nodded. Two years, five months, and twenty days. Not that she was counting.

Gregory gestured to the study. "Your mother is having a call with her new agent. She should be done soon."

Eden walked over to the stone mantelpiece and fingered a picture frame. Inside was a family portrait, the last one she'd posed for at seventeen. She, Elonora, Gregory, and Izzy were artfully arranged, dressed in color-coordinated perfection, smiling at the camera. Amazing she could have looked so happy when her world had been crumbling into dust. But that's what the Falconers did. Put up a front. Smile for the camera. Izzy's first words had been "say cheese!"

Her head jerked up as Elonora walked into the room. She was perfectly put together as always, dressed in a fresh crisp cotton shirt and tan slacks, her feet in stylish ballet pumps. Elonora still wore her hair in the short pixie cut she had favored ever since her cancer scare several years ago. That had been another season of family drama captured and played out on the reality TV circuit. The short hair brought out Elonora's fine bone structure and large arresting eyes. She stretched out her arms and smiled. "Eden. What a surprise! Wonderful to see you here."

Eden walked up to her mother to receive a hug and an air kiss. "Good to see you, too. You look great."

"Thanks, dear." She touched a lock of Eden's black hair. "You've let your hair grow. Suits you much better than that bob you were wearing last time. So, Izzy's been visiting you?" She turned to her younger daughter. "You should have told us you were going, dear. I'd love to see Eden's new place."

Eden glanced at Izzy, who sat on the sofa, fists clenched in her lap, gnawing her lower lip. She'd better break the news now and get it over with. Drawing it out any longer would just increase Izzy's stress levels. Eden sat next to Izzy and looked up at their parents. "Mum, Dad, we have something important to talk about."

Elonora settled into an armchair and arched an eyebrow. "Oh?"

Eden swallowed. Best to plunge in and get the words out there. "Izzy's pregnant."

The words fizzed in the middle of the room like a giant unexploded bomb. For a moment, her parents sat frozen. Gregory was the first to react. He jumped to his feet, staring at Izzy, face darkening. "What? Who did this? Who's responsible?"

Izzy found Eden's hand and held on tight. Elonora pressed her fingers against her forehead as though she had a painful headache. "Of all the foolish, silly, idiotic, reckless, brainless things to do." She looked up, her dark eyes boring into Izzy. "How could you do this to me, Isolde? I thought you were smarter than that. Don't you know how babies are made? At the very least, haven't you heard about the morning-after pill? How far along are you? There might still be options. Are you at twelve weeks?"

Eden's hand tingled as Izzy's grip grew as tight as a vice. Izzy shook her head. Her voice quavered, but she stared straight at her mother. "I'm not having an abortion. I'm going to have the baby."

Elonora balled her hands into fists and stared up at the ceiling, jaw clenched.

Gregory moved over to the sofa and sat on Izzy's other side. "You still haven't told me who is responsible for this. Did... did someone hurt you?"

"No. It's my boyfriend. His name is Kieran."

Gregory scowled, but he kept his voice calm. "You have a boyfriend? Didn't we discuss this and agree you were not to mess about with boys until you were done with your A Levels?"

Izzy's gaze dropped to her hands. "I'm sorry."

"And who is this Kieran?" Elonora asked, her question slicing through the air like a knife.

"He seems to be a good boy," Eden said. "I met him just before we came here. He's very involved with his church."

"A good boy?" Elonora's voice dripped with sarcasm. "How good can he be when he's getting girls pregnant? What kind of good church boy goes sneaking around with a girl behind her parents' backs?" She stood and stalked to the French windows, her arms tightly crossed.

Eden glanced at Izzy. A tear rolled down the girl's cheek. Eden held up her hands. "Listen, it's done. The baby is coming. We need to think about what we're going to do."

Elonora whirled around to face her younger daughter. "And that's another thing, Isolde. You knew we had this project all lined up. The production crew is ready to start filming in just a couple of weeks. What are we supposed to tell them now? All those months of hard work setting this up down the drain."

Eden stared at her mother. On learning that her teenage daughter was going to have a child all Elonora could think about was some reality show? Of course. She wasn't dealing with any ordinary mother. This

was Elonora Falconer, reality TV star.

She got her voice under control before speaking. "Yes, I suppose a lot of plans will have to change. But I meant we need to think for a moment about the practical things and what Izzy is going to need." She squeezed her sister's hand.

Elonora sighed. She raised her phone and thumbed the touch-screen. She held it up to her ear. "I need to speak to my agent. We'll have to tell the production crew straight away." She walked out of the room.

Eden shook her head, letting her breath out slowly. Elonora hadn't changed at all.

Gregory turned back to Izzy. "This boy, is he going to take responsibility?"

Izzy nodded, wiping away another tear. "Yes."

He put his arm around Izzy, and she leaned against his chest. Eden sat watching them as Gregory held Izzy for a long moment. Elonora wore the pants in the Falconer home, but Gregory's heart was mostly in the right place. He loved his daughter, no doubt about that.

Eden's heart squeezed while she looked at them. Her own dad had

taken off while she was an infant, and Elonora had remarried when Eden was eight. She'd called Gregory "Dad," since then, but she was acutely aware that he wasn't really her father.

Gregory was a decent guy, and perhaps the only one who could hold Elonora somewhat in check. Although Elonora's first concern was always publicity and self-promotion, once the first shock was past, Gregory could be sensible about this and put his daughter first. He hadn't intervened in the past when Elonora and Eden had clashed, but perhaps since Izzy was his flesh and blood, he would take a more central role in supporting her.

Eden stood. "I think I'll be heading back to Basildon now. I've got a long drive."

Izzy got up as well, and Eden held her shoulders, looking into her face. "If you need anything at all, I don't care what time of day or night it is, call me. Okay?"

Izzy nodded, and the sisters embraced.

Eden said bye to Gregory and headed toward the front door. As she walked by the study, Elonora's voice filtered out of the open door. She was talking a mile a minute, presumably to her agent. Outside a

moment later, Eden opened her car door and slid inside, pausing for a few seconds before turning the ignition. It was done. She'd helped Izzy break the news to her parents. She prayed Izzy would get the support she needed. Now she could step back to being a big sister.

Chapter Seven

Two months later

EDEN RAN a final spell check on the proposal document she was working on. She had a good feeling about this pitch. Business had been going well for her videography company, especially over the last two years since they had snagged a huge client who then sent plenty of referral work their way.

They were now in the fortunate position of being able to pick and

choose which jobs to pitch for instead of scrambling for work and taking whatever they could get.

She smiled as she clicked the "save" button. The days of getting paid in exposure instead of in cash were long gone, thank God. Perhaps she hadn't made it in her mother's estimation, but she was a success by anyone else's definition.

Eden glanced at her watch. It was well after six o'clock. Where had the time gone? She was supposed to meet Geoff for dinner tonight. It was a date motivated more by guilt than by desire.

She sighed as she closed the apps on her laptop and shut it down. At the dinner party with his friends several weeks ago, she'd known she needed to clarify things with him.

But there never seemed to be a good time to bring it up. Perhaps they could have that conversation tonight. It might make things awkward since he was a silent partner in the business, but that had to be better than the danger of stringing him along.

She needed to leave soon, but she had to call Izzy first. Since Izzy had reached out to her, Eden had made it a habit to check in with her sister every day.

Izzy answered after two rings. "Hello?"

"Hey. How are you doing?"

"Okay, thanks. A bit sleepy, but the midwife says that's normal. She said I should feel more energetic soon."

"Have you had a checkup lately?"

"Yes, I had an appointment today. Kieran came, too."

Eden smiled. From all her conversations with Izzy, it appeared Kieran was remaining fully involved. She hadn't seen him since that brief encounter at Grace Community Church, but she sensed this boy was a keeper.

Or, at least, as much a keeper as a seventeen-year-old could be. "What else did the midwife say?"

"She was happy with my progress. I'll be having my twenty-week ultrasound scan next week."

"That's exciting," Eden said. "Will you find out what you're having?"

There was a smile in Izzy's voice. "I kind of wanted to find out, but Kieran would rather wait. He says I can find out if I want to, but he wants to have the suspense. So, we decided we'll wait until the baby comes."

"You're so patient," Eden said. "I would definitely want to know as soon as I could. And how is school going? Still keeping up with your friends?" The week after Izzy had told her parents, she'd stopped going to her exclusive private school and was working with a home tutor until the baby came.

"The new tutor's like Attila the Hun, but I like him," Izzy said. "He's working me really hard so I don't lose any ground when I have to take a break."

Izzy had made no mention of her friends. Eden frowned. It was probably a struggle to fit in with her schoolmates now that her life had taken such a drastic turn. And, from other things Izzy had said, it seemed Kieran was her best friend, and had been for quite a while. "That sounds good," Eden said. "It'll

Milla Holt

be like having your own personal
coach."

"Yes, if my personal coach was a
cross between Genghis Khan and
Shaka. And when production starts,
we'll have to see how to fit in tutor-
ing hours."

Eden's antenna went on alert.
"Production? Production of what?"

Izzy sighed. "Didn't I mention it?
I'm going to be on a TV show."

"What?" Eden sat up in her seat.
"I thought the show you were supposed to be on was canceled."

"It was. But mum's new agent
asked around and found there was
an opening for another show. He

sent in my video application and they thought I'd be perfect for it."

Eden gritted her teeth in an effort to keep her tone even. "What show is that?"

"It's about teen mothers. They'll follow me through until I have the baby."

Anger bubbled inside Eden. How could Elonora think it was a good idea to put Izzy through the stress and exposure of a reality show when the girl was already dealing with so much? She took a deep breath and swallowed down the rant she'd love to unleash. "Do you know which production company you'll be working with?"

"Hang on. I'll grab the paperwork they sent and check." Half a minute later, Izzy said, "Blue Dragon Productions."

Eden frowned. She'd heard of Blue Dragon Productions. They were known for their hard-hitting drama-filled reality productions. They would go after all the high emotional moments. What was Elonora thinking? Of course, Eden could guess. Having Izzy on a highly rated reality show would probably boost Elonora's own profile and give her leverage on whatever angle she was working lately. What would it be now? A book deal? A cosmetics line? Vitamin supplements? Elonora's business interests were satellites powered by the exposure of her TV appearances.

"When does production start?" Eden asked.

"I think Mum said they'll be beginning preliminary interviews next week."

That soon? Eden's mind raced. "Izzy, I know a bit about this company. I don't think they're unethical or anything, but they want drama and will probably ask you some pretty tough questions, trying to provoke a reaction." There was silence on Izzy's end of the line. Eden asked, "Would you like me to be there with you during the filming?"

"Oh, wow, could you?"

The eagerness in Izzy's voice made up Eden's mind in an instant. "Yes, I'll be there. I just need to arrange some things here at work. But I'll try to come down to Hatbrook within the next day or two."

"Thanks, Eden. I was actually a bit worried about it all."

"Not a problem. I'll see how to reschedule some work, and we'll talk later. I'm sorry, I need to go. I have to meet someone soon."

"Okay. Bye. Thank you so much."

"Bye. Speak to you soon."

Eden tapped her fingers on her desk. She'd made an impulsive promise to attend the filming sessions with Izzy. Now she needed to figure out how to do it. She walked across the open plan office to where her business partner Ruby sat, tapping at a keyboard with her blue lacquered nails.

"Hi, Ruby. Can I have a quick word?"

Ruby looked up at her. "Sure, no problem."

"Conference room?"

Eden didn't want anyone overhearing their conversation. She closed the conference room door as

Ruby took a seat at the large glass meeting table.

Eden sat opposite her, but hesitated. None of her colleagues and friends knew about her family background. When she'd moved away from Hatbrook, she'd changed her surname by deed poll, using her middle name as her new surname.

Everyone who'd met her since then knew her as Eden Tracey. It was her way of putting her past behind her and controlling her own narrative. The last thing she wanted was to be associated with her family, the B-list reality TV stars whose private business was splashed all over the screens.

But how could she frame her request to Ruby without giving all the details? Finally, she said, "I have a family emergency that will require me to be close to my family for a while. "

Ruby's blue eyes widened. "An emergency? I hope everyone is okay."

"It's not that kind of emergency. I can't really go into any details, but I'll be needed at the family home for a while. I don't want to take time off work, so I was thinking I'll keep working remotely."

"Okay." Ruby frowned. "We'll need to shuffle some things around. Any idea for how long?"

Eden did some mental calculations. Izzy was nineteen weeks along. If the filming was going to carry on until she had her baby, she would need to be close to Izzy until then. "About five months."

Ruby's eyebrows flew high above her trendy tortoiseshell glasses. "And you want to work fully remotely?"

"I could probably do a couple of on-site things and be available to come in for the occasional meeting. But, yes. Apart from that, fully remotely. I could take a lot more of the editing and scripting work and some admin." She spread out her hands. "I know it's a big ask, Ruby.

But I wouldn't ask unless I really needed to."

Ruby smiled. "Isn't that why we wanted to be our own bosses? So we can have more flexibility when stuff like this happens? We can make it work if we swap some responsibilities. Can we talk a bit more and figure it out?"

Eden returned her smile. "Awesome. Thanks!" She glanced at her watch. "I need to leave now because I'm meeting Geoff. But we can brainstorm tomorrow about how to shift the task load around."

Ruby nodded, reached out her hand and squeezed Eden's. "We'll work something out. Don't worry."

She tilted her head. "And, um, how are things going with Geoff?"

Eden's stomach quivered with unease. She'd better make it clear to Ruby that there was nothing between her and her brother. "Things? There are no things. We're just meeting for a meal."

Ruby stared at her, head tilted, but didn't comment.

Eden stood. "I'd better go." She walked out of the conference room and went to fetch her bag. It was clear that Ruby wanted to know more about her need to stay in Hatbrook and her friendship with Geoff, but Eden couldn't bring herself to explain.

She had grown a habit of keeping her family life strictly under wraps. Ruby was probably her closest friend, but Eden kept a lot from her. She knew little about Eden's family and nothing about the horrendous choices Eden had made after she left home, in her first year at Bournemouth University. By the time they'd gotten closer, Eden's life had been on a more even keel. She'd held onto and perfected the Falconer legacy of keeping up appearances and managing exactly what parts of herself and her life she wanted to be seen.

Eden shut her computer down and shrugged on her coat. She'd

have to hurry if she was going to make it to the restaurant in time.

Chapter Eight

EDEN WALKED through the restaurant doors a few minutes late. She paused and glanced around, taking in the ambiance. An abundance of flowers and greenery exploded against the wood-paneled walls, and an enormous log fire burned in an open fireplace in the corner of the dining room.

She was definitely underdressed in her belted denim shirt dress.

The maître d' greeted her with an elegant bow. "Good evening, madame. Do you have a reservation?"

"I'm meeting Geoff Gallagher."

"Of course. Come this way."

Geoff was sitting at a table close to the fireplace. He stood, remaining on his feet until she settled into her seat.

"I'm really sorry I'm late," she said, but the guilt that assailed her ran far deeper than her showing up twenty minutes after their date was supposed to start. Geoff wore an impeccably cut suit, while she hadn't even bothered to freshen her makeup.

Geoff smiled. "That's okay. Ruby gave me a heads up you were on your way."

Eden looked up. Ruby had told him? She looked around. "This is a beautiful place."

"It is. The waiting list is months long to get a table here."

"That long? Wow." Eden shifted in her seat, her conscience needling her. He valued her enough to bring her to a place like this? She needed to make it clear she felt nothing more than friendship for him. But how could she do that without sounding like a presumptuous jerk?

The conversation limped along for a while as they ordered and ate

their starters. After the waiter
cleared the plates away, Geoff leveled his gaze at Eden. "When were
you planning on telling me you're
leaving town?"

Eden stared at him.

"Ruby told me," he said.

Eden opened her mouth. Why
couldn't she tell him why she was
going? It would take only a few
words to explain about Izzy, about
why she needed to be with her sister. Geoff had shown himself to be
a caring friend. But the words
would not pass her lips.

As far back as she could remember, her every private moment had
been captured by cameras and

beamed onto TV screens. Her mother had welcomed reality show cameras along when she took Eden shopping for her first bra.

Elonora had even found Eden's diary and read it aloud on camera, letting the country know of her then-thirteen-year-old daughter's first crush. Eden had never kept a diary since then. The minute she had a choice, she had guarded every private thought she could keep a hold of.

There was only one person— Noah—to whom she had been able to completely open up. And even he had let her down in the end.

Geoff was still looking at her. But the habit of keeping her shield up was too hard to break, even when Geoff demanded an answer. The silence spun out into an unbearably tension-filled eternity.

Geoff sighed, pushing his hand through his dark hair. "Listen, Eden. I've not made it any secret that I hoped our friendship would lead to something else. We've known each other how long? Two years? And after all that time, I still feel as though I hardly know you. You're so remote and closed off. I'd hoped we could be closer than friends, but sometimes I question if we even are friends because I feel you've never let me in. Is it something I've said or done wrong?"

Eden shook her head. "No, absolutely not. It's not—"

Geoff held up his hand. "Don't tell me. You're going to give me the 'It's not you, it's me' spiel." His lips twisted in a thin smile. "I guess it's time I admitted to myself that this just isn't going to happen, is it?"

Eden forced herself to hold his gaze. She owed him an honest answer about this, at least. "No. I'm sorry."

Geoff sighed. "I'm sorry, too. I hope you don't mind if I leave early. I'll take care of the bill." He stood and dropped his napkin onto the table. He took a step away, then turned back to Eden. "I care about you a lot. If you ever decide you need a friend, I'll be here."

Eden clasped her hands together and bowed her head as he walked away. She should never have let this thing with Geoff spin out for so long. He wanted more from her than she could offer.

He'd called her remote and closed off. She did protect her inner space. It was precious to her after growing up with reality shows mining deep into her personal business for entertainment material.

After Noah, she'd tried one other time to open up to a man who

seemed to care. But that had been the worst mistake of her life. She'd sacrificed her values for the promise of love and intimacy. But after taking what he wanted, that man had tossed her aside, shattering her heart. Geoff was right to walk away from her. She had nothing left to give.

Chapter Nine

NOAH HELD his cell-phone to his ear, trying to find a small chink in the wall of words into which he could winkle his way and end the conversation. But Mindy, the mother of one of the teenagers in his youth ministry, would not let him in. This so-called dialog was a one-way street.

He drummed his fingers on his office desk.

Mindy was a perfectly nice lady, and she was raising a great child on her own. But Noah had the distinct impression that Mindy wanted to develop more than just a pastoral relationship between them.

He'd visited her and her thirteen-year-old daughter at their home a few months ago, which was something he did about once a year with all the young people under his care.

A week later, he'd run into Mindy and her daughter at a restaurant. His father had canceled a lunch meeting at the last minute, and Noah had made the perhaps unwise decision to join Mindy at her table.

Since then, she'd called regularly, wanting to chat, and had invited him to go out with her. Noah politely declined each invitation, keen to curtail any expectations before they could take root.

He'd had two serious relationships with women in his life. Both times, it had ended in crushing heartache. The lingering shadow of pain reared its head whenever the fleeting thought of dating crossed his mind. No. He would not start anything with Mindy.

He glanced up as Kieran appeared in the doorway.

When Mindy finally paused for breath, Noah grabbed his chance. "I

have to go now. Someone's here to see me."

"Oh, okay, Pastor Noah. It's always lovely to talk to you. You're so encouraging."

Noah's lips twisted in a smile. Encouraging? He'd barely managed more than a couple of words. "Thank you. Goodbye."

"Speak to you soon. Bye, now."

Noah ended the call and switched his phone to its "do not disturb" setting. He looked up at Kieran and smiled. "Hey there."

Kieran pointed a thumb over his shoulder. "Your secretary said you might be busy. Do you have a couple of minutes?"

"Of course, I've got a couple of minutes." The secretary he shared with the associate pastor knew that Noah kept this time ring fenced for his own personal study. Her instructions were not to let anyone interrupt him, apart from a short list of people, which included Kieran. "Grab a seat and tell me what's on your mind."

Kieran sat in front of Noah's desk. "Well, it's like this. Izzy's going to be in a reality show about teenage parents."

Alarm bells went off in Noah's head, but he held his tongue and nodded. Best to hear Kieran out before spouting an opinion. All he

knew about reality shows was what he'd heard from Eden.

The Falconer family were regular fixtures on the TV circuit. Eden had hated it, but perhaps Izzy felt differently. He wouldn't have thought a reality show was the ideal place for her to be while coping with all the issues she had going on, but who was he to judge? Maybe Izzy enjoyed being in front of the camera.

Kieran went on. "The producers of the show approached me and asked whether I want to be a part of it, since Izzy is having my baby."

Noah wasn't sure he liked the direction this was taking. "Okay."

Kieran rubbed his forehead. "I don't know whether it's a good idea. But they said they'll pay me if I do it, and what they're offering will come in really handy. It would help with my college tuition and maybe also to get a couple of things for the baby."

"What does your uncle think about this?" Noah asked.

Kieran shrugged. "He says I'm almost an adult and he'll go with whatever I decide."

"So, have you decided?"

Kieran nodded. "I'm going to do it."

Noah paused before he replied. Eden used to talk to him about what

she hated most about being on a reality show. She couldn't stand the invasion of her private space.

He looked at Kieran. "Are you sure you're ready for your life to be put on TV? You'll be fair game for all sorts of stuff. People will talk about you on social media, picking apart what you say, making snap judgments about you. Some of it might even make it into the press."

Kieran frowned. "Even if they say nonsense, that'll just be words, right? I promised Izzy I'd stand with her. If she's going to be on TV, I don't want people thinking she's some baby mama who hooked up with a random guy who doesn't care about her. I want them to know I love her and I'm stepping up. The money is a welcome bonus since I could really use the cash. But the main reason I'm doing it is because I want Izzy to know I've got her back."

Noah stared at the young man in front of him. This kid was something else. And people said chivalry was dead among the Zoomer generation. "That's a very noble attitude. I'm proud of you for thinking like that."

Kieran grinned, his face flushed. "Wow, thanks! I'm not trying to be noble or anything. I just love Izzy. Isn't that what you do when you love someone? But I wanted to ask you a favor. Since I'm still a minor, at least in the legal sense, the production company said I could bring a responsible adult to be with me while they're filming."

Noah stroked his chin. "That sounds reasonable."

"So, I wanted to ask whether you could be there when they're filming me. I would have asked my uncle, but he's so busy."

Noah smiled at the unspoken implication that he was any less busy. What did people imagine a pastor did with his time? He put the thought aside. As Kieran's pastor and mentor, he was committed to supporting him, especially now. "Of course I'll attend the filming with you."

Kieran pumped his fist. "Thanks so much. It'll make a huge difference knowing that you're there."

Noah's heart warmed. "Not a problem. Any idea when the filming will start? I'll need to mark the times in my calendar."

Kieran frowned. "Yes, of course. I forgot to tell you. The first filming date is tomorrow afternoon."

That soon? Noah opened his planner and flipped through the pages. "I'll see if I can free up some time. Let me know as soon as you find out any other times you'll be needed."

Kieran stood. "I'll do that. Thank you so much, pastor."

"No problem. See you at youth group?"

Kieran grinned. "I wouldn't miss it."

Kieran left the office, and Noah stroked his chin. After hearing so much from Eden about reality shows, he was finally going to get a peek into that world. Her world. Or, at least, the world she'd been raised in. He had no idea what she was doing now. The woman he'd glimpsed weeks ago at his church was a stranger, not the girl who'd been his best friend.

If reality shows were anything like Eden had said, Kieran would need his support. He stared at his planner and picked up his phone. He had to reschedule some commitments if he was going to spend tomorrow watching Kieran get filmed.

Chapter Ten

EDEN SAT in a red leather booth at the Hatbrook bowling alley, watching as a TV production crew fussed around Izzy's hair and fixed her makeup.

It was the first week filming the reality show High School Mum, and the crew wanted to capture footage of Izzy and Kieran out on a bowling date, after which they would record on-the-fly interviews with the two of them. The production crew had completely engineered the date.

They, and not the teen couple, had suggested the venue and the time. But Kieran and Izzy would have to act and talk as though nobody was watching.

While the crew carried on with their setup, Eden grabbed the chance to check her emails and phone messages. Working remotely had been going okay over the past week. She was present whenever Izzy was being filmed and fitted her editing work and admin tasks for her clients around the filming schedule.

After making it clear where she stood with Geoff, it was a relief not to have to see Ruby at the office.

Ruby was a professional, but Eden had noticed a shift in tone following that last date with Geoff. Either Geoff had put a spin on things, or Ruby had been more invested in the potential relationship than Eden had realized.

Distance was a good thing, because she and Ruby could more easily keep their focus on work. The Geoff issue would go on the pile of topics they avoided. She opened her email software, breathing a silent prayer for Geoff. He was a nice guy. Hopefully, he'd soon find someone who could return his feelings.

Eden scrolled through her emails. A couple of them needed attention fairly soon. She could use this time to deal with those. She typed and sent a response to the most urgent one, then glanced up.

Kieran was walking into the bowling alley, Noah following close behind. Her heart rate picked up. What was Noah doing here? A member of the production team rushed forward and shook the men's hands. She touched Kieran's shoulder and led him off to where the hair and make-up team were working on Izzy.

Noah stood by himself, rubbing his jaw and looking around the hall.

His eyes snagged on to Eden's before she had a chance to pretend to look elsewhere. Her hand shot up of its own volition and smoothed her hair.

He hesitated for a moment, then walked up to her booth. "Things are really busy around here."

"Yes, there are a lot of moving parts."

He made a sweeping motion with his hand, taking in the crew. "They all seem very professional."

"From everything I have heard, they have a pretty good reputation in the industry."

Noah turned to face her. "You're familiar with the industry?" A tinge of pink touched his cheeks. "Dumb question. Of course you know a lot about all this, after all the shows your family has been on."

"I work in videography myself, and it's a fairly small world."

His hazel eyes widened. "Really? I didn't know you were interested in that."

His surprise didn't shock her. He of all people understood her ambivalence to the whole reality TV industry. In the past, she'd often complained to him about what it was like to have cameras everywhere.

She smiled. "It sounds like a strange career choice for me, but one of the TV production crew working at our house once got to talking to me about the work they did. I got interested in being behind the camera instead of in front of it." She gestured around her. "And as far as reality shows go, these guys are doing everything by the book. Trust me, I've checked."

Noah's head bobbed up and down. "That's encouraging. I wasn't so sure it was a good idea for Kieran to be part of this. Mind if I sit down?"

"No, go right ahead." She scooted farther up the booth, making room for him. He took off his coat, and she suppressed a smile at what he was wearing underneath. His acid-green hand-knitted sweater pictured reindeer and snowmen frolicking across a wintry landscape. His grandmother used to send him a new sweater every Christmas, and Eden guessed this was one of her creations. Grandma Chaplin was a skilled knitter, but her sense of color was way off. But Noah had always worn the hideous sweaters faithfully, and it looked as though he still did. He sat down, laying his coat next to him.

"Have you known Kieran long?" she asked.

Noah rested his elbows on the table. "About four years. He moved to

Hatbrook to stay with his uncle after his mum died, and he's been part of the youth group since then." He looked at Eden. "He's a good kid. I know you're probably wondering about that."

"That's encouraging to know." Eden had tried to find out more about Kieran from Izzy, but she wasn't sure she could entirely trust her sister's opinion, given how besotted she was with the boy. To hear Izzy tell it, Kieran practically walked on water. Having Noah vouch for him eased some of Eden's worries.

She turned to watch the crew prepping Izzy and Kieran. The hair and make-up artists had done wonders. Izzy and Kieran were already attractive, but the team had added subtle tweaks that made them resemble a pair from a movie poster.

She looked at Noah. "I think it's a good sign this crew has allowed Izzy and Kieran to have a responsible adult sit in on the filming. Before they finalized Izzy's contract, they wanted to be sure she could handle the pressure of being on their show. They had their psychologist evaluate her, and they needed a written go-ahead from her midwife. I think they'll try to do right by them."

Noah nodded and turned to watch the crew at work. Eden grabbed the chance to study his profile for traces of the boy she'd once known. A few strands of silver shot through his dark hair. He might be like his dad, who'd gone gray early. What had been going on with him over the past years?

He caught her looking at him, and heat rose up her neck. "Kieran mentioned Izzy was going to Basildon to see you. Is that where you live now?"

"Yes. Although I'll be in Hatbrook for a few months while Izzy's doing this show."

He picked up a pen from the table and played with it. "Been in Basildon long?"

"I moved there about a year ago. I used to live in London."

He put the pen down and leveled his gaze at her. "Did you lose my phone number?"

Her blood turned to ice. "What?"

"You dropped off the face of the earth and I never heard from you. Did you get a new phone or something and lose my contact details?" He stared at her, arms crossed.

Heat flooded Eden's face and neck. She had gotten a new phone with a new number and hadn't imported his. Cutting off contact with

him had been a deliberate choice. "I... I just—"

The floor manager called for silence, and Eden exhaled. She had a few minutes' grace to think up an answer if he repeated his question. There was no way she could tell him the real reason she'd ghosted him.

At first, it had been simple enough, though still too embarrassing to share. She'd realized her feelings for him went far deeper than friendship. He'd just gotten engaged to Angela, and seeing them so happy together was a painful reminder that he saw her as nothing but a friend.

Then, after she'd started a physical relationship with her ex and made some other poor lifestyle choices, she'd been ashamed to get in touch with Noah. She'd hated the thought of him discovering just how far she'd strayed from God.

Even now, when her life was back on track and her faith deeper and stronger than ever, her heart still ached with regret and shame about the year she'd backslidden. Perhaps it was her ego, but she wanted to cling onto the good opinion he'd had about her. She couldn't bear to sink in Noah's estimation, to watch the shock and disappointment in

his face if he ever found out. Especially since he was a pastor now.

She would leave if she could, but she needed to be here for Izzy. And moving to a table away from Noah would look strange. She'd just need to figure out a generic answer if he asked her again, and hope he didn't probe any further.

She watched Izzy and Kieran as they bowled for the cameras. The teens were stiff at first, then relaxed as they got going with their game. Eden sneaked a glance at Noah. He was watching everything with open fascination. What had happened with him and Angela? Why hadn't they gotten married? Was she still in his life? She was burning with curiosity, but if she asked him, he might want some answers of his own from her about why she hadn't kept in touch with him. Better to keep that door firmly closed.

During a break in filming, Noah turned to look at her. "Why did they ask Kieran to walk up to Izzy and say hi after they'd already been bowling for half an hour?"

The tension inside Eden uncoiled a fraction. Thank goodness he'd dropped the question about her ghosting him. Videography was her bread and butter, and she could answer questions about it all day long. "They'll switch things around in the edits. The order in which stuff is filmed has no bearing at all on where it'll appear in the show. After all this, they might even interview Kieran and have him answer questions as though he hasn't seen Izzy yet. Stuff like, 'Are you looking forward to your date?' Or 'When's the last time you saw Izzy?'"

He quirked an eyebrow. "Not exactly spontaneous, is it?"

"No, it isn't."

"So, why do they do that?"

Eden shrugged. "Lots of reasons. Sometimes—"

The producer called for silence again, and the cameras rolled for Izzy and Kieran's on-the-fly interviews. The teens stood side by side, fingers interlocked. Eden smiled. They looked so cute together. The producer started with softball questions about how they had met and what Kieran did.

After a couple of minutes, the questions got a little more hard-edged. The interviewer turned to Kieran. "Do you think being a father will get in the way of you having fun?"

Kieran shrugged. "The most fun I have is when I'm hanging out with Izzy, and I hope that won't change."

The interviewer probed some more. "Don't you like chilling out with your mates? Going to parties? Won't a baby cramp your style?"

"I don't do that kind of stuff much, anyway."

The producer looked up from her clipboard. "Try to include my question in your answers because I'm going to be edited out. Let's try that again. Won't a baby cramp your style when you want to chill out with your mates or go to parties?"

Kieran rubbed his chin. "I don't do much partying and I've never been one to idle around with my guy friends, anyway. So, the baby won't interrupt something that wasn't happening in the first place."

The producer turned to Izzy. "Most people say having a child completely changed their relationship, and not always in a good way. You're obviously really close right now, but do you think being a mum will change things between you and Kieran?"

Izzy glanced at Kieran and smiled. "I don't know how things will change between us. We'll just try to take everything as it comes."

"Statistics say that most teen relationships don't last any longer than two years, and most people have between ten and twelve relationships before they get married. So, the odds of you still being together

in three years' time are really slim. What do you say to that?"

Eden gripped the edge of the table and leaned forward. The question had lurked in the back of her mind, although she'd never have put it so bluntly. On paper, Kieran and Izzy stood little chance of staying together for the long haul. They were both young and had so much growing to do.

Izzy frowned. Her hand drifted to her stomach, resting on her small but noticeable baby bump. "I try not to live by the law of averages. I've always been taught to do my best. And if my best doesn't work, at least I'll know I tried. I think if you go into something thinking you're going to fail, it makes it more likely that you will. I'm not afraid of working hard, and I know Kieran feels the same."

Kieran nodded vigorously. "Obviously, it's not going to be easy, but I'll put in the work I need to. My pastor says relationships aren't about putting in fifty-fifty. He says both of you need to put in one hundred percent if you want it to work. I'm in this a hundred percent."

Eden glanced at Noah. He was listening intently to the teens, hands folded in front of his face. Was he the pastor who'd given Kieran that advice? Had he given one hundred percent to Angela? If he had, why weren't they married now?

The questions went on, and Kieran handled himself well, speaking fluently. The camera was going to love him. Finally, the floor manager called for thirty seconds' silence so the crew could capture room tone. When that was done, she announced the session was a wrap.

Noah turned to Eden. "So, that was it?"

"Looks like it."

His shoulders relaxed. "Maybe there isn't much to be worried about if that's as tough as it gets. I thought Kieran did pretty well."

"He did amazingly well. He came across as natural and sincere. If he was nervous, I didn't catch it at all."

Noah nodded. "I think he's on top of this. But he asked me to attend all his filming sessions, and I'll do that as long as he needs me around."

Eden's heart thumped. That meant she would see him again. She wasn't sure whether she liked or dreaded the idea.

Chapter Eleven

AFTER FILMING wrapped for the day, Kieran and Noah had to leave immediately so Kieran could catch a class. As they left, Eden allowed herself to relax. She'd avoided answering Noah's blunt questions. For now.

Eden hugged her sister. "You did great. How did you feel out there?"

Izzy smiled. "Glad it's over. Hey, do you mind if we stop at the mall? I'm desperate for some new jeans.

Mine don't fit anymore, and even the rubber band trick barely works now."

Eden paused as she packed up her tablet. "The rubber band trick? What's that?"

"I read about it on an online mummy magazine. You loop a rubber band into your buttonhole and use that to fasten the button. It means you can do up your jeans even though your tummy's getting bigger."

"Oh, that's clever," Eden said. She glanced at her watch. She had pressing deadlines, but Izzy's bump was visible now, and she needed some maternity clothes. "Okay, let's

go, but I can't stay more than an hour."

Fifteen minutes later, they walked into the trendy clothing boutique Izzy had picked. Eden glanced around at the impossibly thin mannequins dressed in up-to-the-minute fashions. Did this place really have anything as boring and practical as maternity wear?

A shop assistant strode up to them, as bouncy and cheerful as the pulsing music filtering through the store. "Hi, ladies. Anything I can help you with or are you just happy to browse?"

"Where's the maternity wear section?" Izzy asked.

The shop assistant smiled. "Right this way." She led them toward the back of the shop, speaking to Eden over her shoulder. "We've just got a shipment of a fantastic new clothing line designed exclusively by Skylar Martin. She included some maternity pieces, and I think you will love our selection." She gestured at several dresses and blouses hanging on racks. "Any questions, just give me a shout." She smiled again at Eden and walked away.

Eden glanced at Izzy. Even with her TV-ready hair and makeup, she was unmistakably a teen. With Izzy's coat hiding her bump, no wonder the lady assumed Eden was

the one looking for maternity clothes.

"So, jeans, wasn't it?" Eden pointed to a row of shelves where folded maternity jeans lay stacked in high piles. "Look, they have two types. Some that go over your bump and others that sit under it. What kind are you after?"

Izzy picked up a pair of dark blue pants. "The mummy magazines say you should try both types and see what you're most comfortable with. Apparently, some women hate the feel of the fabric against their bumps."

Eden stared at her. The world had gone topsy-turvy. Her little sister, who a few short years ago was obsessed with Barbie and Ken dolls, was now discussing maternity wear with more knowledge than Eden herself had. She shook her head to bring herself back to the present. "Okay, let's grab both kinds, and you can try them on and see which you prefer."

Izzy walked between the shelves, reaching out to touch a pile of black jeans. "So, you and Noah seemed to be having a cozy chat at the bowling alley." She looked up at Eden. "How did you say you knew each other?"

"We used to be friends a while ago. Best friends, actually."

Izzy's eyebrows drew together. "If you were best friends, why did you lose touch? Didn't you say you haven't heard from each other in about eight years or something?"

Eden shrugged, putting an effort into making her voice sound breezy and nonchalant. "It happens. I moved away from Hatbrook and got busy studying. People lose touch all the time."

"Not if they're best friends." Izzy tilted her head and continued to study Eden's face. "Did you have a falling out or something?"

"No." Eden walked toward a rack of hanging clothes. "What about tops? Don't you need maternity tops as well?"

Izzy held up a finger. "I know. Were you in love with him?"

Eden whirled around to face her. She forced out a laugh that she hoped showed Izzy that her guess was beyond ridiculous. "In love with him? What gave you that idea?" She reached out for a pair of gray jeans and held them up in front of Izzy. "I think these would look great on you. Shall we add them to the pile?"

Izzy took the jeans but didn't drop her gaze. "What gave me the idea you were an item? I don't know. It would explain why you hadn't been in touch with your best friend. But I guess you didn't treat him any different than you did the rest of us."

"What do you mean?"

Izzy slung another pair of pants over her arm. "I mean, you dropped contact with all the rest of us."

Izzy didn't raise her voice, but her words were like shards of glass. Eden winced as they cut deep. "I never meant to lose touch with you. I just had to get away from... from a bunch of stuff."

"You even changed your name." Izzy put her hand on her hip. "I saw it on your mail in your flat. What was that about?"

Wasn't this girl ever going to let it go? Eden sighed. "It was just about having a clean break. I didn't want everyone to associate me with 'the Falconers'." She raised her hands and made air quotes. "Just for my own sanity, I wanted a fresh start."

Izzy looked at her for a long moment, then sighed and dropped her gaze. "Yeah, I know what you mean."

Eden reached out and touched her shoulder. "I didn't handle things well. Believe me, I know that. But I'm here now. I won't lose touch again. I'm sorry I missed so much of your growing-up years. But

I'm determined to be around for you now."

"I get that," Izzy said quietly. "Sometimes I wish I could just get away, too."

Eden pulled her into a hug. Izzy was dealing with a lot more than she'd ever had to handle.

Izzy leaned on her for a moment, then stood back. "I'd better go try on these jeans. You said you only had an hour, right?"

"Take your time." Eden followed Izzy to the fitting room. "If you need a second opinion, just give me a shout."

Izzy disappeared inside with her armload of clothes, and Eden glanced at her phone. A couple of emails had come through from clients.

She'd have to stay up late again tonight to stay on top of all her work. But she had no intention of going back on her promise to Izzy. Even though she risked running into Noah and facing even more awkward grilling sessions, she'd stay here as long as Izzy needed her.

Chapter Twelve

EDEN SIGHED and tapped her foot. Why did she always pick the wrong supermarket checkout? When she'd joined the queue to pay for her hand moisturizer and lip balm, she'd been certain she'd be done in no time.

The only people in line ahead of her were a heavily tattooed teen and a man in a business suit, each carrying just one small shopping basket with a handful of items.

But a situation had developed, and all forward movement was frozen. The besuited man was engaged in a long debate with the cashier about a potentially expired coupon. Things escalated until the manager was called.

Eden threw a glance over her shoulder. Several people stood in line behind her, and it would be a pain to squeeze past all of them and their shopping carts. She would just have to wait.

The manager finally pulled the irate customer aside so the queue could keep moving. Why hadn't he done that in the first place? The

cashier smiled apologetically as she scanned Eden's shopping.

When she had finally paid, Eden headed toward the exit.

"Eden! Is that you?"

Eden spun around. A woman in a power suit with professionally styled gray hair walked toward her. Eden's face grew warm as she recognized Rachel Chaplin, Noah's mother.

"I thought it was you." An enormous smile lit up Rachel's face. "I knew my eyes weren't playing tricks on me. As I live and breathe, Eden Falconer! It's so good to see you." She threw her arms around Eden.

Eden returned the hug. "Good to see you, too."

"It's been so long," Rachel said. "I'm just about to have a coffee. Do you want to join me? We could have a quick catch up."

A refusal flew to Eden's lips, and she stood poised to make her excuses and leave as quickly as possible. But Rachel had always been kind to her, and her enthusiasm was heartwarming. Eden smiled. "Thank you. I'd love to."

They headed to the supermarket café, where Rachel ordered a Café Americano and Eden got a skinny latte. Both of them resisted the tempting sweet treats on offer, and

they took their drinks to a round table in the corner.

Rachel settled into her chair. "It's so good to see you. How long has it been? Five years? No, it must be more than that. I haven't seen you since before Noah got ordained."

Eden sipped her drink. "I think it's at least eight years." She knew exactly how long it had been, but wasn't about to display her precise knowledge.

Rachel nodded. "You might be right. I haven't seen you since before that horrible business with Noah and Angela. It was terrible. You must have heard about it."

Eden shook her head. "I only found out fairly recently that they didn't get married."

"No, Angela ended things with him just days before their wedding. It was such a big shock, although perhaps we should have seen it coming. Noah was absolutely devastated. And that's when we really noticed you hadn't been around. He could have used a friend back then."

Guilt twisted Eden's gut. She tried to think of something to say, but Rachel continued speaking. "I thought you must have moved abroad. I think Noah tried to reach you. I asked whether he'd been in touch with you, but he said he didn't have your contact details. I assumed it was just male pride, not wanting to talk about everything that happened with Angela."

Two women came up to the table, causing Rachel to stop short. One of them, tall and thin with her salt-and-pepper hair scraped into a bun, spoke to Rachel, but her eyes were on Eden. "Hello, Mrs. Chaplin. How are you?"

Rachel smiled a thin smile. "Hello, Mrs. Grant, Mrs. Smith. This is Eden Falconer, an old friend."

The women smiled at Eden and murmured their greetings. Mrs. Grant said, "Falconer. I thought there was something familiar about you. You wouldn't be related to Elonora Falconer from the telly?"

Eden managed to get out a yes, then Rachel burst in quickly. "We won't keep you waiting, ladies. See you on Sunday."

She watched the women walk away, then faced Eden and leaned forward. "Being a pastor's wife is like living in a fishbowl. They can't contain their curiosity and want to know who I'm with and what I'm doing all the time. I can't be doing with such gossipy people."

She sat back and sipped her coffee. "Anyway, I was still telling you about Angela. She led Noah a merry dance, that one. He practically turned himself inside out trying to make her happy. I don't like to interfere, but I did wonder. The only thing he wouldn't compromise on was becoming a pastor. She didn't want him to, and she wouldn't budge. They were both very young, but they had a lot of support and we had all gotten used to the idea of them getting married.

"But a week before the wedding, Noah called us and said Angela didn't want to go through with it. He'd set his ordination date and I guess it finally dawned on her that he was serious about becoming a minister, and he wouldn't enter some other line of work."

Eden stared at her. "So, that's why Angela broke it off? She didn't want to be a pastor's wife?"

Rachel nodded and took a sip of her coffee. "She didn't want to be a pastor's wife, and she didn't want him to be a pastor. They're slightly different reasons, but in Angela's case, it was both."

She tapped her chin. "Although perhaps she was wise to end things when she did. Not everyone is cut out to be a pastor's wife. Everyone's eyes are on you, and they all want to know your business. You saw those ladies who were just here. It's going to be over the sewing circle that I've been having a coffee with Elonora Falconer's daughter. Perhaps it was a good thing Angela left when she did."

She made a face. "But she should have given him the ring back. That is just so not classy to keep it. £8,000, that ring cost. I think Noah is still paying for it."

Eden shook her head, trying to make sense of all these pieces of the puzzle. Her heart ached for Noah. She'd never imagined Angela would do that. "And this happened after they'd been engaged, what, two years?"

Rachel nodded. "Exactly. A two-year engagement, only to break it off on the eve of the wedding. That's what I gather from the little he's told me. She wasn't ready to be married to the church." Rachel's voice lowered, and she spoke almost as though to herself. "She could have handled it better, but I can't say that I blame her. Noah was gutted, of course. He just buried himself in his youth group. He lived and breathed for those children, and he's done a tremendous job. And as if that wasn't enough, he got his heart broken all over again by that Charlotte girl."

Eden swallowed. "Who was Charlotte?"

Rachel scowled. "She had us all fooled. Such an innocent face, carrying on as though butter wouldn't melt in her mouth. Turned out she'd been living a double life, having an affair with the new bass player in the church band. He was married, mind you. The two of them eventually ran off together. It's taken a while to heal the trouble that all caused."

Eden was silent for a moment. Two devastating breakups, on top of dealing with the fallout of adultery between church members.

That must have torn Noah's heart to pieces. "That's awful."

Rachel sighed. "We've had some dark years. It didn't surprise me that Noah quit dating for a long while." Her face brightened. "But things are looking up now. Don't say you heard it from me, but one of the teens in his group has a lovely, widowed mother, and I think there might be something brewing there."

Eden arranged her features to mirror the smile on Rachel's face. "Really? Wow." A lead weight settled in her gut. Of course, there was a woman waiting in the wings to patch up and heal Noah's broken heart. What could be more natural than Noah meeting somebody at church? He was eligible. And according to Izzy, there were lots of unattached women available.

Might things have been any different if she'd stuck around and remained friends with him? Maybe their friendship might have blossomed into something more after Angela left him.

But who was she trying to kid? Noah had never seen her as more than a friend, not even when they were very close and hung out together a lot. And what were the odds he'd ever look at her now? She had a past. One that was hardly appropriate for a pastor with a gossipy congregation. Not to mention a gossipy, if friendly, mother.

Rachel slapped her forehead. "Oh my, I haven't even asked what you're up to. What are you doing with your life? And what brings you back here?"

"I'm a videographer. I have a small business making films for clients." She hesitated, unsure whether to tell Rachel about Izzy's pregnancy. Eden's instinct was to conceal, not reveal things. But the pregnancy wasn't exactly a secret. Izzy was filming a whole TV show proclaiming it to the world. "I'm staying in town for a while because

my little sister is pregnant, and she needs my support."

Rachel's eyes grew round. "Your little sister? She can't be much more than, what, fifteen? Sixteen?"

Eden nodded. "She'll be seventeen this summer."

Rachel squeezed her hand. "It's wonderful of you to come here and support her. I always knew you had a heart of gold, and I wondered why you and Noah never—but never mind. I'll keep you all in my prayers."

Heat rushed to Eden's face. What had Rachel been about to say? "Thanks. I appreciate that. We'll need prayer."

"The baby is just the beginning, of course. Any plans of what will happen afterward? Where will the child live? What about your sister's education? What was her name again? No, don't tell me. I know this. Irene? No. Isabelle?"

Eden smiled. "Close. Isolde, but everyone calls her Izzy."

"Izzy," Rachel repeated. "Well, you'll definitely need a lot of prayer." She checked her watch. "Look at the time! I'd love to talk some more, but I've got to run. By the way, have you seen Noah since you came into town?"

"I've run into him a couple of times." A stab of disappointment hit her chest. Noah hadn't mentioned to his mother that he'd seen Eden? That put things into perspective.

But what was she expecting? She'd bailed out of their friendship, so it shouldn't surprise her that her return wasn't worth telling his mother about.

Rachel patted her hand. "You know where we are. Look us up sometime. In fact, I'll just get your number right now." She pulled out her phone and swapped numbers with Eden. "I'm off. Please don't be a stranger."

The two women hugged, and Rachel walked away. Eden sat back in her chair, lost in thought.

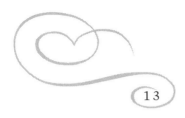

Chapter Thirteen

NOAH STEERED his ten-year-old Toyota Corolla through the large iron gates of the Falconer home. He pulled to a stop, parking his humble set of wheels between a white BMW X5 and a black BMW M4 cabriolet.

In all the time he'd been Eden's best friend, she'd never invited him to her home or met her parents. It hadn't seemed strange to him at the time, since she'd once told him she hung out with him to avoid spending time at home.

Now, bringing Kieran to film footage for High School Mum, he was seeing the home Eden had grown up in for the first time.

A member of the TV production crew met them and hustled Kieran away. A security guy glanced at the tag Noah had clipped to his coat and waved him inside the house. Noah looked around him. There was no doubt about it: the Falconers had exquisite taste and a lot of money with which to indulge it.

He walked through the hallway, jumping aside as a crew member

barreled past him with an armload of equipment.

"You'd better sit over here so you don't get bowled over."

Noah looked up. Eden waved at him from a large doorway. He did a double take. Wearing a black turtle-neck sweater and tan slacks, her black hair piled on top of her head, she looked as though she belonged in this stylish house. She was a poised, sophisticated woman, a world away from the pony-tailed schoolgirl he'd once known.

But her smile was as warm as he remembered. He followed her into a bright living room, and she gestured toward a group of chairs in

the corner. "You won't be in anyone's way there. They're supposed
to be filming a family dinner, so all
the attention is going to be centered
on the dining room."

"Thanks," he said, taking off his
coat. "Is it like this every day? The
filming, I mean."

She shrugged, a small crease
forming between her eyebrows.
"It's been pretty busy lately.
They've been getting footage of a
lot of Izzy's hobbies and activities.
Her instrument practice, study sessions with her tutor, visits with the
midwife, chats with Mum and Dad.
They won't use it all, of course, but
they want to film several hours'

worth and decide what will best fit the story."

"Story?" Noah asked. "I thought this was reality?"

"Oh, there's always a story." Her tone had an edge, and he sensed there was a lot behind her words. "They'll decide what aspects of Izzy's life to emphasize. Could be her extra-curricular activities, her family life, her academic prospects, her relationship with Kieran. And then they'll tailor and tease the footage to bring out the angle they want to show. My guess is today they'll be exploring how Kieran interacts with the family and seeing whether there's a story there."

"Are you going to be part of the show?"

Eden stared at him. "Me? Absolutely not. Those days are behind me." She half turned. "Can I get you a tea or a coffee?"

"Tea, please."

She left through an arched entryway on the right and he sat back, taking in the rushing crew. Everyone was busy. A woman taped down the cables that snaked across the floor, while two men peered into their hand-held cameras. Nobody gave him more than a passing glance.

Eden brought his tea and left again. A pang of disappointment hit

him as he watched her go. It would have been nice to chat with her. There was a lot he wanted to know. Like, why had she shut him out of her life for so long?

The room suddenly filled up as Elonora Falconer came in, followed by her husband and a couple more people from the production crew. Noah sat up a little straighter, but Elonora marched past him and into the dining room. His gaze trailed after her.

She was a stunning woman, even more beautiful in person than on TV. Eden had inherited her height as well as her facial features. But the resemblance stopped there.

Elonora's expression was hard and unsmiling, as though molded from golden brown topaz. When she spoke to one of the crew, her voice was too quiet for Noah to hear, but the crew member's face reddened as the younger woman scurried to the dining table. Noah thought the table settings looked good enough to be on a magazine layout, but the woman began to move some things about.

Izzy and Kieran walked in holding hands, and Noah caught Elonora's lip curling as she looked at Kieran. Oh boy. Kieran might be in for a rough time.

The producer, a woman Noah recognized from the filming session at the bowling alley, walked into the middle of the living room. She spoke with a raised voice. "Okay, people, we're almost ready. If you four wouldn't mind getting around the table, we'll start with dinner. Keep the conversation natural. I might prompt you to talk about a specific topic but act as though we're not here, okay? Where's the food?"

A woman wheeled a trolley laden with food out from the kitchen and set the serving platters onto the table. The smell of grilled chicken wafted toward Noah, and his gut growled. It had been a while since lunch. He sipped at his tea.

Izzy, Kieran, Elonora, and Mr. Falconer took their places around the table under the glare of the large bright lights that were rigged up close to the high-vaulted ceiling.

As the producer called out more instructions, Eden slipped back into the living room and sat in an armchair. Her posture was rigid, and her eyes were fixed on the group at the table. Noah frowned. Why did she look so tense?

The producer called for silence, and filming began. Elonora handed the dishes around and the four people at the table helped themselves to the food. After some banal chitchat, the conversation lagged. The floor producer spoke up.

"Kieran, why don't you speak about some of the things you've been learning about childcare?"

Kieran nodded, then turned back to the table. He cleared his throat. "I was reading something interesting today about baby wearing. You know, carrying your baby around in a sling or a carrier. I think it would be a great thing to try." His eyes slid to Izzy, and she smiled encouragingly at him.

Elonora sipped a glass of water. "Is that a fact? What did you learn about baby wearing?"

"Um, I read that it's a great way for a baby and his parents to bond. There is this theory that gestation lasts eighteen months: nine months before birth and nine months after. So, in the nine months after, baby wearing is supposed to help the baby feel secure and warm and helps them to regulate their body systems and feel close to their mother."

Elonora listened, one eyebrow raised. When Kieran was done, she tapped her chin with a well-manicured finger. "So, let me get this straight. You are advocating that Izzy spends nine months with a baby on her hip?"

Kieran fidgeted in his seat. "Well, they recommend the baby be held as much as possible while the mum is going about her regular tasks."

Elonora's voice dripped with sarcasm. "So, Izzy is supposed to put her studies and the rest of her life on hold for nine months in order to walk around carrying a baby because you think it's a good idea?"

Heat rose up Noah's neck and he clenched his fists.

Kieran, bright splashes of red on his cheeks, glanced at Izzy, and she looked back at him, eyes wide. Kieran looked back at Elonora. "Dads can do babywearing, too. I just thought it would be a good thing for the baby."

Elonora folded her arms. "Let me ask you something, Kieran. Are you supporting Izzy in any way financially? Are you paying for the roof over her head? Are you supplying her with any of the many things she needs? Food? Clothes? Supplies? Health care?"

Kieran's entire face flamed red. He shook his head. "No."

Elonora sliced into a piece of chicken. She turned her eyes away from Kieran as though he were not worth any further attention. "Well, I suggest that when you start to pay, you can start to give advice."

A hot wave of anger washed over Noah. How could Elonora so ruthlessly rip into Kieran like that? She had dismissed him as though he was a complete nobody.

A movement to his right caught his eye, and he turned as Eden jumped to her feet. Fists clenched, her face like a thundercloud, she stepped toward the production manager and whispered into her ear.

The woman began speaking, but Eden cut her off, stabbing a finger toward the dinner table. The production manager grasped her headset and called out, "Okay, everyone. Let's take a short break."

Kieran stood and left the table. He walked toward Noah, his lips trembling, a sheen in his eyes. He dropped into a chair opposite Noah, his head hanging down.

Noah leaned forward. "Hey, you did great, okay?"

Eden came up and touched Kieran's shoulder, crouching down so they were at eye-level. He lifted his head to face her, taking a deep breath.

"Hey, Kieran. Don't let any of that get you." She spoke quietly, her gaze intent as she looked straight into Kieran's eyes. "You are that baby's father, and you have every right to an opinion about how he or she is raised. Don't let anyone try to tell you that you don't."

Warmth washed through Noah. This was the Eden he remembered. How many times had she come up with exactly the right thing to say to him when he'd been struggling?

Kieran nodded at Eden, his eyes filling up. He wiped a tear away with the back of one hand. Eden gave him a quick hug before walking away.

Noah squeezed Kieran's shoulder. "Hey, she's right, you know."

"Thanks," Kieran said. Izzy walked up to them and sat in the third seat, slipping her hand into Kieran's.

Noah looked up. Elonora sat at the table next to her husband. Her face was perfectly serene, as though she was completely untouched and unmoved by the hurt she had just caused.

What kind of woman was this? He understood now some of the things Eden used to talk about. He looked at Kieran again. The boy and Izzy spoke quietly to each other, heads close together. Poor Kieran. Was he ready for such a mother-in-law?

Chapter Fourteen

A FEW WEEKS later, Eden ran a duster over the oak display cabinet in the dining room. It was a relief to have a quiet day with no filming. She'd woken up early to give the living and dining room a deep clean. More importantly, without the hassle of a filming session, Izzy could have a rare day to relax.

The Falconers had a cleaner who came in twice a week, but this wasn't one of her days, and Eden wanted to get started on the spring cleaning. Cleaning was an incredibly cathartic task. The act of putting things in order, whisking away clutter, removing grime and dust, calmed her. She was in control of her physical environment, and could make it look as perfect and regimented as she wanted. Life was messy, but at least she could make the things around her neat.

Eden turned her duster to the heavy oak sideboard, then looked up at the sound of quick-stepping heels on the hardwood floor. Elonora stormed into the room, holding up her cell phone. "What's the meaning of this?"

Eden straightened up. "The meaning of what?"

"I just saw this email from Blue Dragon Productions, saying they're happy to postpone filming because they agree that Izzy needs a day off. Did you do this?"

So that's why Elonora was upset. "Yes, I told them Izzy was feeling a bit run down, and she needed a day off from filming."

"And who appointed you to make a decision like that?"

Elonora's tone needled Eden. "Someone has to think about Izzy and the baby."

Elonora's eyes narrowed. "Oh, and I suppose that would be you."

Eden put the duster down, willing herself to calm down. Elonora was trying to pick a fight. When she was in that type of mood, it was best not to play into her hands. Eden took a slow, deep breath before replying. "I think we can all agree that Izzy's health and well-being have to take first place, ahead of the TV company's production schedule. They see it the same way, too."

Elonora took a couple of steps forward. "And what do you think the reason is for this whole production? This is for Izzy's sake. It's a great opportunity for her after we had to cancel the other show. That's

why I went through the trouble of making it happen. The situation isn't ideal, but I'm trying to make the most of it."

Eden shook her head and picked up her duster again. In her mother's view, "making the most" of a situation meant finding the best camera angle, or the catchiest elevator pitch for a new TV show. "That's all well and good, but I could see how tired Izzy was. She's been running herself ragged trying to keep up with the work her tutor has given her on top of hours of filming every day. She hasn't been sleeping well and, oh yes, one little detail: she's sixteen and having a baby." Eden could not keep the sarcasm out of her voice.

Elonora's eyes glittered. "Do you think you have the right to decide what's best for my daughter?"

"No, it's not about having a right to do anything." Eden held her hands up, palms outward. "It seemed to me Izzy was struggling and needed a day off. I was just trying to keep her best interests in mind. She's got a lot on her plate."

Elonora crossed her arms. "We haven't seen you in years, and now you show up and step in—no, interfere—in Izzy's life. When she was on track, doing better than you ever did, collecting all those awards and recognition, you were nowhere to be found. But now you're all over her business. What did you come back for? To gloat because it looks like her life has hit a roadblock?"

Eden's throat tightened as her mother's words lacerated her. She gripped the back of a chair so hard that her hand went numb. "No, absolutely not. I'm not jealous of Izzy. I'm here because she wanted my support, and I promised to look out for her. And that means making sure she gets rest if she needs it. She's having a baby."

Elonora slammed a fist into the back of a dining room chair. "I will not let this pregnancy derail her life. This is the best way to make lemonade out of lemons and make sure she stays on track and still has opportunities to make something of herself."

"But she shouldn't have to do it at the cost of her health. And there are other ways of making opportunities than being on TV."

Elonora's eyes narrowed. "You've always felt as if all this is beneath you, haven't you? Well, these reality shows you despise have paid for this house and for the fancy education that you had. Although you have very little to show for all the money we've spent on you. You went and botched your admissions interview at Oxford, and you've gone downhill ever since, ending up in this nothing job of yours. What is it you do, film weddings and christenings? Are you trying to make sure Izzy ends up in a dead-end career rut like you? Just because you've made nothing of your life, that doesn't give you the right to ruin Izzy's chances. Don't you dare do anything like this ever again."

Elonora turned on her heel and left the room.

Eyes burning with unshed tears, Eden looked up and saw Izzy standing in the doorway, wide eyes fixed on her. Behind her stood Noah and Kieran.

Chapter Fifteen

NOAH, FROZEN in the entryway, watched as Elonora spewed a torrent of ugly words. Eden stood rigid, flinching once as Elonora jabbed a finger close to her face. Elonora turned and stalked past the group without a backward glance. Noah's gaze flew to Eden's face.

Her eyes widened as she saw him, then her features twisted into an imitation of a smile. "Didn't you guys get the memo? There's no filming today."

"I guess they forgot to tell us," Noah said.

Kieran shuffled his feet. "It's probably my fault. I haven't checked my email."

Izzy took a step toward her sister. "Are you okay?"

Eden nodded. Her eyes were unnaturally bright. "Yeah, of course. I've got a bunch of work to finish up here. Why don't you guys use the extra time to chill out? Go do something fun."

Izzy frowned. "Are you sure?"

"Of course. Go."

Izzy looked at Eden for a moment, then turned to Kieran. "I'll walk you outside."

The teens headed to the front door.

Noah followed them, but hesitated as Izzy pulled on her coat. Elonora's blistering words still rang in his ears. "Why don't you guys go ahead? I'll be along in a couple of minutes."

Kieran and Izzy left through the front door, and Noah stood in the hallway. A clock chimed, but the house was otherwise quiet. Eden had insisted she was fine, but he'd seen her face, heard what her mother had said. It was none of his business, but he couldn't leave without making sure Eden was really okay. He went back into the living room.

Eden still stood in the dining room, her back to the entryway, a bright yellow duster in her hand, swiping away at a spot on the table.

Noah took a step closer. "Eden."

She gave no sign she had heard him. She bent her head lower and continued to wipe the table. The duster whipped back and forth, a yellow blur against the deep brown wood. Noah walked forward until he was a few feet away.

Her back still toward him, she said, "I've just got to make sure I finish cleaning this place. Incredible how dusty it gets." She continued swiping at the sparkling table, her hands making twitchy robotic movements, like a broken puppet.

Noah walked forward until he was right next to her. It had been years since they'd been close, but the connection was still there. He could sense her pain. She used to come to him when she needed to escape from home. Sometimes just hanging out was enough, other times they'd spend hours talking when she wanted to get stuff off her chest.

He didn't know who she went to now, but his gut told him she needed a friend. Right now, in this moment, the vast gulf of silent years didn't matter. All that mattered was she was hurting.

Without a word, he covered her hand with his, stilling the frantic motion. Her head still down, she turned and leaned against him. His pulse quickened. He wrapped his arms around her and held her tightly as sobs ripped their way out of her body.

Chapter Sixteen

EARS POURED out of Eden like a raging waterfall she couldn't control. The sound of her own ugly hulking sobs horrified her and she couldn't stop that, either. Shame mixed in with her pain, and she didn't know which emotion was worse.

Noah had heard everything, witnessed her mother humiliating her. He stood firm, one arm tightly around her, stroking her hair with his other hand.

Finally, she got some control back and gulped back a sob. She was vulnerable and exposed, desperate to pull the tattered shreds of her dignity together and cover herself. "I'm sorry," she said, wiping at her eyes with the edge of her sleeve.

Noah didn't reply, but pulled a pack of tissues out of his coat pocket and handed it to her.

She fished one out and blew her nose, unable to bring herself to meet his eyes. Why was he still standing there? When would he go away and leave her to piece her mask back into place so she could pretend nothing had happened?

But instead of going, he spoke. "Hey, I've got an idea. Why don't we go do something fun?"

Surprise overcame her embarrassment, and she dragged her gaze up to meet his. "What?"

"Let's just drop everything and go play hooky."

She shook her head. "Are you serious?"

"Completely serious," he said. "Hang on a minute."

He walked out toward the hallway, and she wiped her eyes again. What was he talking about? She caught sight of herself in a large silver punch bowl in the cabinet. Her face was puffy, her eyes red and swollen. Oh, great. She was a complete mess, and long overdue for a hair appointment, too. She smoothed her hair back with her hands and dabbed at her nose.

Noah came back in. "I've spoken to Izzy and Kieran. They're going to hang out and he'll find his own way home. Come on, let's go."

She looked at him for a moment, all the things she still had to do flashing briefly past in her mind. Cleaning the living room, putting together a client proposal, a stack of admin work Ruby was waiting for.

Suddenly, she laughed. "Okay, let's do it."

He grinned back at her. "Awesome! Let's go."

She followed him into the hallway and pulled a coat over her sweatshirt. Walking through the door he held open for her, she asked, "Where are we going?"

He smiled. "First, food and caffeine."

They rode in his car to the mall and went into the Roasted Bean Café. The welcoming smells of roasted coffee and freshly baked goods caressed Eden's senses, and she decided her day of hooky would extend to calorie counting. She was going to have the most sugar and carb-laden item on the menu.

They found a free booth against the back wall. Eden pulled off her coat and as she sat down Noah said, "Wait a minute here. I'll be right back."

She leaned forward, resting her elbows on the table. The pain from her mother's words still lingered, a fresh ache to add to the deep pool of residual hurt that had built drop by drop over the years. She brushed her fingers against her upper arms, remembering how Noah had held her.

He came back to their booth, holding a large colorful box, which

he set down in the middle of the table. "Boom!"

She laughed. "Legos? Where did you get that? I thought you'd gone to order our coffee."

"From the toy shop next door, of course. I thought we could build this fire station set while we have our snack."

She grinned. He'd been mad about Legos, even as a teenager, and they'd spent many hours putting together constructions and chatting. "You mean build it right here?"

"Of course. What do you want to order?"

Eden answered without hesitation. "A full fat caramel latte and a double chocolate muffin, please."

"Coming right up. Why don't you get started with the Legos while I bring our drinks?"

He headed toward the counter, and she examined the box of Legos. This was totally crazy. She had a ton of work to do, and she knew that pastors were usually really busy as well. Yet here she was in a coffee shop about to play with Legos with Noah, of all people.

But she was absolutely going to do it. She'd live in the moment and sort out the consequences later. She

opened the cardboard box and laid the contents onto the table.

There were two instruction books, so she started with the first, putting together the frame of the fire truck. Noah came back, carrying a tray with two mugs of coffee and two chocolate muffins. Lego pieces were spread all over the small table, so he handed Eden her drink and food before setting the tray onto an empty table next to them. "I see you made an excellent start. What do we have here?"

She sipped her latte, enjoying the blend of the sweet caramel and bitter coffee against the rich milky base. "Mm, this is so good! I'm doing the things in the first booklet, so you could make a start on the fire station."

"Sounds like a plan." He bit into his muffin. "These are absolutely delicious. Still warm, too. And, look, there's a gooey bit in the middle."

They ate in silence for a moment while she allowed the sugar and chocolate to work their magic. It was a short-term fix, resolving none of her problems, but being away from home and her responsibilities, sharing a sweet treat with Noah, was like a soothing balm to her pain. She wiped the crumbs from her mouth and looked at him.

"Thank you." She meant for more than the muffins and coffee, and she knew he understood.

His smile crinkled the corners of his hazel eyes. "Let's get on with this."

They worked on the Lego set, building in silence for a while. That was another thing Eden had forgotten about Noah: how, with him, there was no need to fill the air with chatter. She missed having a friend like that. Noah knew everything about her. Well, not quite everything. She pushed aside the thought of the only part of her life he was unaware of, those dark lost years just after she'd left Hatbrook and turned her back on him, her faith, and her values.

Noah clipped a red brick onto the emerging fire station. "After we're done here, do you want to do something else? Like maybe go sightseeing to MacArthur Fort?"

Eden smiled. "I haven't been to MacArthur Fort in years. Remember the last time we went there? When you were pretending to be a tour guide?"

Noah grinned. "Yes, and I had that group of Japanese tourists following me around for half an hour."

Eden cracked up. She struggled to speak through her laughter. "And you were telling them about how

King Wilfred Wipesnot had his traitorous cup-bearer executed for not saying bless you when he sneezed."

Noah chuckled. "The poor fellows actually believed me. But I repented! I felt sorry for them and told a genuine tour guide they had some questions."

They both laughed until tears came and Eden's stomach muscles ached. Gasping for breath through peals of laughter, she said, "What, so you want to go back there and play fake tour guide again?"

Noah shook his head, smiling. "No, I'm a pastor now. I wouldn't dare do that. Someone might recognize me."

They looked at the Lego fire station they had built, complete with a tower, fire truck, and even a small dumpster fire for the little firefighters to put out. "It seems a shame to dismantle it," Eden said. "Maybe we can carry it without breaking it?"

"We could do that. Or, wait, I've got another idea." He went to the counter and came back with a large paper carrier bag. Together, they lifted the fire station and placed it inside. "I'll pass it on to the Sunday School coordinator. The children play with Legos before the lesson starts, and they might like this."

When they'd cleared away the Legos, Noah looked at Eden. "I've got the afternoon free if you want to make a full day of our little French leave. Want to go bowling?"

A fleeting thought of her work made barely a blip on her conscience. She nodded and smiled at him. "Only if it's my treat this time."

They bowled a couple of rounds, splitting the victories between them. After that, they were starving again, so they ate an early dinner at the Nandos restaurant next door. Eden looked at Noah across the table. He was checking the messages on his cell phone for the first time since they'd left her home. He hadn't mentioned her mother once or referred to what he'd walked in on. No judgment passed, no questions asked. He'd just been exactly what she needed today: a friend.

She smiled, enjoying the warmth of the moment, hugging it to herself, savoring the feeling. But it couldn't last forever. It was time to go. He looked up, catching her gaze on him, and quirked one eyebrow.

"I've had the best time today," she said. "But I guess we can't play hooky forever."

He smiled back. "Unfortunately not. I've had an amazing day, but I've got to attend the evening service. Dad's preaching, but there might be people who need counseling or prayer support. Have you got a bunch of work you need to catch up on?"

"I need to put a draft proposal together for a project we're pitching to get. My business partner is expecting it tomorrow. I can just about finish if I pull an all-nighter."

He made a face. "An all-nighter? Sorry, I should have let you go earlier."

"Don't be silly. I stayed by choice. And it was worth it."

He grinned. "Awesome. Come on, I'll take you home."

His car pulled up into the driveway of the Falconer home, and he turned off the engine. She turned to look at him and her hand found his, squeezing it tight. He held hers in his warm grip.

"Thank you so much," she said quietly. "For everything."

"Let's do it again sometime. I'd forgotten how much fun it was to hang out with you."

She didn't trust her voice to reply, so she nodded and let go of his hand, then climbed out of his car.

She remembered exactly how much fun she'd had with him in the past, and how he used to be her safe space whenever she needed to get away from the pressures of home. He'd been that again today. She had

to be careful, though, because a whole lot of other old feelings about Noah were rushing right back, too. She remembered exactly why she'd fallen in love with him, and her heart was hurtling once again down that well-trodden path. It was a dead end, though, a road that ended in heartache. Was being close to him again worth the pain of knowing he didn't love her back?

She waved as he drove his car away.

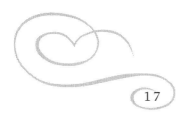

Chapter Seventeen

EDEN SAW Noah several times over the next couple of weeks. He came to Kieran's filming sessions, and the days he showed up were the highlight of her week. They'd maintained the comfortable footing they'd shared since the day they'd played hooky, although they steered clear of personal questions.

He'd not asked her again about why she'd ghosted him, and she hadn't broached the subject, either.

Perhaps this was the new normal, having Noah at arm's length, exchanging surface-level banter. She missed the old closeness, but she couldn't have that deeper connection again without exposing things in her heart and her life that she wasn't willing to share.

With the invisible walls between them, they didn't have the same friendship they had in the past, but she was enjoying the connection they had. It would have to be enough.

Today, she'd given in to Izzy's pleas and agreed to attend the Sunday service at Grace Community Hatbrook.

Eden spent way more time than usual choosing an outfit for church. She finally settled on a purple cowl-necked wool dress that skimmed her body and flared out from her hips to her knees, creating the illusion of a slimmer waist.

She teamed it up with knee-high boots and styled her dark hair into a knot at the nape of her neck. Examining the effect in her mirror, she nodded with satisfaction. Even camera-ready Elonora would approve of how she'd put herself together today.

When they got to Grace Community, Izzy made a beeline for Kieran, who was hanging around

the church entrance. Eden followed them to their seats near the back of the church. She scanned the gathering congregation. Would she recognize anyone from her time here before? Most of the faces were unfamiliar, but there were a few she knew. Several of them gave her a double take.

Pastor Chaplin's rich voice was the same as she remembered as he gathered everyone together in an opening prayer. His hair was completely silver now, and the lines in his face a lot deeper.

Eden gave herself over to the service, immersing herself in the singing. Pastor Chaplin chose the parable of the unforgiving servant as his text.

"Think about the enormous debt we all owe to God. Not one of us can ever hope to pay it back. And yet God forgives us completely. And then, like the servant in this parable, we turn around and refuse to forgive the pennies somebody else owes us."

The words cut deep into Eden's heart. She bowed her head, her thoughts flashing to the lifestyle in which she'd lost herself after leaving Hatbrook. Nobody here knew about the string of anonymous hookups, the way she'd treated herself and her body like trash because she'd felt worthless. God had wiped the slate clean, and she thanked Him for that every day. She was completely forgiven and more solid in her faith than ever.

But just as she'd received forgiveness, she needed to forgive her mother. After her big blowup, Elonora had acted as though nothing had happened. Izzy's schedule remained as packed as ever, with Elonora even asking the tutor to come in a couple of extra hours a week. It was as though Elonora were making a point to Eden: Izzy is my child, and I can do what I want.

She needed to forgive her mother, but it was hard when

Elonora showed not the slightest sign of remorse for anything she'd said or done. Izzy didn't even get Sundays free. Elonora insisted she study for a couple of hours after church. After that, the two of them would go over Izzy's social media calendar for the next week, put together by Elonora's publicist. With a minimum of three daily posts on four platforms, it took up almost the entire day.

"When the show hits, people will look you up," Elonora had insisted, when she'd come up with the plan to have Izzy's social media professionally curated. "There'll be a lot

more traffic, so we want to be ready."

The service ended, and the congregation began milling around. Eden looked up at the sound of Rachel calling her name. Noah's mother, standing at the front of the church, grinned and waved at her. Eden walked over to Rachel. Next to her was an attractive woman wearing a silk dress that emphasized her knockout curves.

Rachel hugged Eden. "It's so good to see you! How have you been? I had such a great time chatting with you the other day."

Eden smiled. "I've been okay, thanks. That was a great sermon."

Rachel shrugged. "Mm, I suppose. Hey, sorry about the short notice, but if you don't have any plans for lunch, why don't you come over to our place? I've cooked up a storm, so there's plenty."

Eden caught the expression on the face of the woman standing next to Rachel. The woman shot a hard glance at Rachel, her polite smile freezing into a teeth-baring grimace.

Rachel squeezed Eden's arm. "Go on, say yes. It's been ages since you were at our place."

Eden glanced at the woman, whose smile was back in place. She didn't have any special plans for today, since Izzy was going to be busy with studying and whatever else Elonora had lined up. "Thanks, I'd like that. I'll just run Izzy home first, then come over."

"Excellent! Oh, I nearly forgot. This is Mindy." Rachel leaned forward and whispered, "I think I mentioned her when we had lunch. Mindy, this is Eden. She's an old friend of the family."

Recognition sparked in Eden's mind. This was the woman Rachel said had a budding relationship with Noah. Her gut twisted as she turned toward Mindy. "Nice to meet you."

Mindy's lips hardly moved as she spoke through her wide smile. "Great to meet you, too." She turned to Rachel. "My daughter's going to spend the afternoon with the Johnsons, so I'll just make sure she's on her way before I pop over to yours. See you soon, Eden."

Eden watched Mindy go. With her smooth brown hair and blue eyes, Mindy looked a lot like Angela. Was Noah really involved with her? He had said nothing about having a girlfriend. But then things had moved pretty quickly with Angela as well. Eden had hardly had time to process the fact they were an item before they got engaged.

She pulled her thoughts back to the present to catch what Rachel was saying.

"I'll go now and sort out the final preparations," Rachel said, patting Eden's arm. "Looking forward to seeing you."

Half an hour later, Eden entered the Chaplin home, stepping straight into Rachel's warm embrace. "You made it, sweetheart. Welcome!"

Eden followed her into the house, removing her coat and laying it on the huge trunk in the foyer. The delicious aroma of a stew mingled with the unmistakable fragrance of freshly baked bread. It was like stepping into a time machine. The Chaplin home was just as she remembered it: cozy and welcoming, with lots of wood and earth tones. For several years, this house had felt far more like home to her than the Falconer place.

Pastor Chaplin welcomed Eden with a large grin and a firm handshake. "Hello, Eden. It was wonderful to see you at church today, and it's even better to have you back in our home."

A rush of warmth flooded Eden's heart as she looked into Pastor Chaplin's eyes. She blinked back the sudden moisture in her own eyes. "Thank you. And that was a

moving sermon. It really made me think."

He squeezed her hand. "I'm glad you found it helpful."

Noah stood up from the fireplace where he'd been tending a small crackling blaze. It was supposedly spring, but the cold snap they'd been having made the fire very welcome. "Hey, Eden."

Mindy walked in from the kitchen. An apron covered her silk dress, and she held a large stew pot. She looked very much at home. "I'll just set this on the table, shall I, Rachel?" Her words were addressed to Rachel, but the full beam of her smile was directed at Noah.

"That's right, dear," Rachel said. She turned to Eden. "Let's all sit at the table while I grab the rolls."

Acting by habit, Eden was headed toward the seat she usually occupied, but a smart maneuver by Mindy meant she had to pivot and choose a different spot. Mindy clearly intended for Noah to have the seat next to hers.

When they were all settled, Pastor Chaplin said, "I just had such a sense of déjà vu with Eden here at the table."

"It feels like old times, doesn't it?" Noah said.

Rachel grinned. "Old friends and new. What a blessing." They joined

hands with the ease of long habit. Thomas said grace.

Rachel pointed at the pot. "Help yourself, Eden. It's my Sunday beef stew."

Eden smiled, scooping up a bowl of the slow-cooked stew, which Rachel made with bacon, mushrooms, and carrots. It was a Sunday staple at the Chaplin home. Eden had eaten it countless times and just the smell of it brought a rush of warm memories.

Thomas helped himself to a bread roll. "I recently met your sister, Eden. She tells me she used to fellowship at St. Matthew's church. She's a lovely girl."

Eden smiled. "Thanks. She loves Grace Community and wants to be more involved. She's quite busy lately, though."

Thomas nodded. "I understand. A lot going on. She's in my prayers."

Mindy looked between Thomas and Eden. "Oh. Anything wrong? I can pray for her, too."

Eden stared at Mindy for a moment before answering. "My little sister is having a baby. She's sixteen."

Mindy's eyes widened. "The little sweetheart! I had my Caroline at eighteen, but I was married. I can well imagine what she's going through. Everyone told us we wouldn't cope, but we made it work. Of course, my dear departed husband was twenty, but that's still young."

Eden listened as Mindy spoke at length about the advantages of marrying young, finishing with, "I guess the big advantage is by the time Caroline is eighteen I'll still be young enough to enjoy life. Are you married, Eden?"

"No."

"Aw. Well, don't despair, darling. There's someone out there for all of us." Mindy flashed a smile at Noah.

Eden stole a glance at him. This woman was coming on really strong. Was he into her? Noah's neck turned red. He didn't reply to Mindy but spoke instead to Thomas. "You'll never guess what I heard just as I was on my way here. The speaker who I'd lined up to speak to the girls at Spring into Life just canceled. She's had a family emergency and can't make it."

Rachel clucked her tongue. "Oh, that's too bad. You've been preparing a while for that."

"The girls are going to be pretty disappointed, too. They'd all been looking forward to this, and we built it up a lot on social media and the church website."

Mindy threw up her hands. "Oh, no! My Caroline is so excited about it."

Thomas shook his head. "That's too bad. It will be hard to find someone at such short notice." He slid a spoonful of stew into his mouth and chewed slowly. Then his eyes widened, and he looked sharply up at Eden. "Wait a minute. What about Eden?"

Eden stared at him. "What?"

Thomas pointed, speaking more enthusiastically. "Eden could fill in."

Noah's face brightened, and he turned to look at her. "That's right! Eden, you would be perfect. If you're not busy, do you think you could fill in and give the girls a talk?"

Mindy's gaze swiveled to Eden. "Are you a speaker?"

At the same time, Eden asked, "A talk? What's this about?"

Noah smiled. "Sorry, we have rather sprung it on you. I was planning Spring into Life, this big event with the girls in the youth group next month. I had a speaker coming to talk to them about navigating through high school and going into college as a young Christian woman. She was going to talk about transitioning to a place with greater freedom and independence when there's nobody from your family or home church to look over your shoulder. I wanted her to talk about withstanding outside pressure, like when your family doesn't support your faith and when your friends and the world around you may not give you that support either. She was going to talk about choices and difficulties and stepping into adult life and holding onto your faith and making a firm foundation of good choices. And Dad is right. I think you would be amazing. You have a genuine gift for communicating. I still remember the great talks you gave when you were part of the youth group."

Eden's heart sank steadily lower with every word Noah spoke. She shook her head. "I'm not the right person to talk about that."

"Think about it," Noah said. "You came to the Lord when you were a teenager. Your family didn't exactly support you, but you were plugged into the church and your faith. You continued growing in your faith and you're still walking with God. I think you have a story these girls need to hear. You've been exactly where these girls are now."

Eden gripped her fork. Where she had been in her late teens was in one of the worst periods of her life, a spiral into darkness that had

begun when she'd realized she loved Noah at the same time he'd fallen for Angela. Also at the same time, the academic dream her mother had pushed her to achieve and work so hard for was falling to pieces. Her whole life had felt like it was completely tanking, and she'd left Hatbrook to get away from her disappointed hopes.

But at university in Bournemouth, where nobody knew her, she'd tried to blank out her pain by getting involved with the first attractive guy who'd shown an interest in her. That had led into a lot of bad choices, until she could barely recognize herself as the innocent church girl who'd come to the university from a small village.

There was no way she could hold herself up as a role model to the girls of Grace Community Church.

She looked at Noah, trying to formulate a refusal. "I'm not qualified to speak about that."

"The more I think about it, the more I think you would actually be a far better choice than the original speaker," he said. "You're actually from Hatbrook, so there is that. Would you think about it?"

Eden hesitated. She did not want to speak to the youth group, and no amount of thinking would change

her mind. Everything inside her re-coiled from doing this.

Thomas nodded. "I agree with Noah. You would do a wonderful job, and you could really help the young ladies."

Rachel spoke up, her voice sharp. "And there it is. The pastoral guilt trip. Laid on thick so you feel like an utter wretch for refusing." Eden stared at her, mouth open in shock. Rachel glanced at her. "Don't feel pressured to do it if you don't want to, Eden. It's your choice, and no is a perfectly legitimate answer." Rachel turned to look at Noah first and then at Thomas. "She doesn't want to do it. Leave it at that."

A heavy silence hung in the room. Eden was stunned by the tone of Rachel's words.

Noah's voice broke the tense stillness. "You're right, Mum. Sorry, Eden. I got carried away by my enthusiasm. Of course, you don't have to do it if you don't want to."

Pastor Chaplin stared at his plate, his face set in grim lines.

Mindy jumped in, her voice bright. "I'm happy to help in any way you want, Noah. I'm not the most qualified either, but I'm willing to learn."

Between the two of them, Rachel and Mindy kept the conversation going, but something had shifted in

the atmosphere. Pastor Chaplin was a lot quieter, and Eden couldn't get over the way Rachel had spoken, as though something simmering below the surface had burst out. The immediate danger of being asked to speak to the youth group was past, and Eden was sure Noah wasn't going to put any more pressure on her.

Still, she counted down the minutes until the meal was over, relief washing over her when it was time to leave.

Chapter Eighteen

NOAH SLID a dinner plate into the dishwasher in his parents' kitchen. He and his father were in charge of the cleanup after Sunday lunch. Rachel had left soon after Eden to attend her weekly book club. Thankfully, Mindy had needed to pick her daughter up, or she might still be here and Noah would have had to entertain her.

He'd been trying to create distance between himself and Mindy.

Seeing her here at his mother's invitation had been an unpleasant surprise. Did Rachel really think he wanted a relationship with Mindy?

He straightened up, hand churning through his hair. Where had the afternoon gone wrong? He'd been delighted to see Eden at church that morning, and her presence at lunch brought warm memories of happier times, when his parents had gotten along better and life was much less complicated.

But this afternoon there'd been a definite false note. It wasn't just Mindy's presence, although her habit of dominating the conversation grated on him. There was something terribly wrong between his parents.

He walked over to the sink and ran a jet of water over the ceramic inner pot of the slow cooker. And then Eden had acted all weird, too. Had it been unreasonable of him to ask her to speak at the girls' event? He didn't think so. Eden had been a regular at Grace Community.

She was a strong Christian, and she wasn't shy. So, why did she resist giving a talk he knew she could do? It was a jarring reminder of the distance between them. He just couldn't figure her out anymore.

He placed the heavy pot on the dish rack and looked around. His father was wiping down the cook-top with a microfiber cloth, but the work was just about done. Noah dried his hands with a towel. "I'll be heading off, Dad. I need to work out how to plug the gigantic hole in the Spring into Life schedule."

Thomas turned toward him, holding up a finger. "I have an idea. If you grab my address book from my study, I'm sure there are a couple of names you could look up. There's a lady I've got in mind, but I don't remember her surname."

"Awesome! That would really help. Where's your address book?"

Thomas gestured over his shoulder. "Should be on my desk."

Noah headed into Thomas's study. He frowned at the clutter. Dad wasn't the best at tidying up after himself, but his house-proud mother had more than picked up the slack in the past. Perhaps she'd grown weary of keeping Dad's things in order. Thomas's thick address book sat in the middle of the desk, partially hidden under a stack of mail. Noah grabbed the book, then paused. A word in heavy dark lettering jumped out at him from a document in a half-open desk drawer. "Divorce."

He slid the drawer open. The document was a form, titled "Application for a divorce, dissolution or judicial separation." Noah pulled the document out of the drawer and leafed through all sixteen pages. Words and phrases jumped out at him, each one a sledgehammer smashing the world he thought he knew. "Your application, known as a petition in divorce and judicial separation." "Do you have a solicitor?" "Give the reason for your divorce or dissolution."

Why did his father have this in his desk?

Gripping the documents, Noah walked into the kitchen where Thomas was wiping the granite-topped island with a pink microfiber cloth. "What is this?"

Thomas looked up at him. "What is what?"

Noah held up the papers. "Why are you looking at this divorce application? What's going on?"

Thomas froze. "Where did you find that?"

"I saw it when I was looking for your address book. Why do you have this?"

Thomas didn't answer immediately. He spread the cloth out on the dish rack. Slowly, he walked over to the kitchen table and sat down, resting his elbows on the rose-patterned wipe down tablecloth. "Sit down, Noah." His voice sounded drained and tired as he

pushed his hands into his hair. Noah pulled up a chair and sat facing him, stomach twisting.

"Your mother and I have been having a rough time for a while. She brought up the idea of a judicial separation, but it may not come to that. We're trying to work through things."

"How can you be trying to work through it when you've got this?" Noah slammed the documents down, harder than he had intended. "You've always taught me that whenever divorce is on the table, it becomes a more likely option. What's going on?"

Thomas made eye contact. "Things have been difficult for a while. Both of us have made some poor choices, but I take responsibility. I made some arbitrary decisions early in our marriage, and things have festered."

Noah frowned. "What decisions?"

"For one thing, I went into full-time ministry as a pastor after we were already married, against your mother's wishes. She had dated and married me when I was on track to a career in the corporate world."

Noah's heart pounded. "I... I didn't know that." It sounded a lot

like the red line that had led to his breakup with Angela.

"Your mother did her best to adjust, but she has struggled. She had no idea I was even thinking about being a pastor. She grew up as a pastor's kid and hated feeling like she was in a fishbowl. The last thing she wanted was to be a pastor's wife. But after we were already married, I felt a calling to be a Pastor. We talked about it for a while, and I felt it was important to obey the call in my life. So, I went through with my studies and came here."

Thomas sighed. "While you were younger and she was taking care of you, that masked a lot of things. But ever since you grew up and left home, it's become clearer that our lives have been growing in different directions. We've been seeking help, but it's not easy."

Noah gestured at the papers, his mouth dry. "But this?"

Thomas sighed again. "I don't think either of us want that. We are praying. But there's a lot to work through."

Noah felt the foundation beneath him shuddering as if it had been rocked by an enormous earthquake. His mother had never wanted to be a Pastor's wife. All these years, she'd been unhappy. He had noticed tensions between his parents,

but he'd never suspected their problems were this bad. A lot of things suddenly made sense. His mother's increasingly frequent out-of-town trips, her reduced involvement in church activities. She still attended Sunday services whenever she was in town, but had given up her ministry roles years ago.

A chill froze his heart as he thought of Angela. The same thing might have happened if he'd married her. She'd been reluctant to get involved in church, too, sometimes turning him down point blank when he asked her to do the simplest things. The way Eden had done today.

He stared at his father. Thomas suddenly looked old and very tired. How had he endured the heartache of knowing his wife was opposed to his life's calling? Noah had been devastated when Angela split up with him. But looking at Thomas, he saw there was a pain worse than that, a daily sorrow which his father had lived with for almost thirty years.

Noah jumped up. "I have to go."

Thomas looked up at him. "I'm sorry you found out like this. But it's not set in stone and we are working it out." He hesitated. "Just pray for us."

Noah nodded and headed for the front door. When he got to his car, he remembered that he'd never gotten the names from his father's address book. But he didn't want to go back and face his father.

In Thomas's face, Noah glimpsed a vision of himself thirty years from now, at the bleak end of a souring marriage. It terrified him. It was far better to remain as he was. He could endure a lifetime of lonely nights. But he couldn't stand the thought of love morphing into bitter disappointment.

Chapter Nineteen

EDEN KNOCKED on Izzy's bedroom door and stepped inside. Her sister sat cross-legged on her bed, textbooks spread around her. Eden glanced around the room, a loft conversion decorated in purples and grays.

A poster of the periodic table hung on one wall, next to a shelf crowded with trophies and medals. On a daybed next to the window, Izzy still had some of her favorite stuffed animals, including a well-

worn Pooh bear that had once been Eden's.

Izzy looked up at Eden, adjusting her glasses on her nose. "Hey."

"Hi. Got a minute?" Eden moved a textbook aside, glancing at the cover as she sat on the edge of the bed. "*Advanced Calculus*, huh? How's that going?"

Izzy shrugged. "Okay, I guess. Mr. Pavlovsky wants me to study at least two hours a day."

"That sounds about right for calculus. Are you able to fit it in?"

Izzy pushed a stray curl off her forehead. "It wouldn't be too bad, except he also wants me to put in two hours a day each of mechanics and organic chemistry. That's besides working through past papers and doing practical work."

"That sounds brutal. Aren't you going to defer your exams?"

"Mum doesn't think I should. She says if I front-load the work now, even if I take a few weeks off in August when the baby comes, I'll still be on track to do the exams in May."

Eden shook her head. "I thought she'd dropped the idea of you taking them in May. You were already a year ahead of schedule, so deferring them would only put you in line with the other students your age."

Izzy shrugged again. "You know Mum."

Yes, Eden knew Elonora. Her mother believed that the best way to get results was to pile on the pressure. She pulled her phone out of her pocket. "I won't take up your time. I just wanted to know when we can interview a couple of doulas."

As eager to help as Kieran was, Eden was convinced that Izzy would need a more experienced and knowledgeable birth partner. They'd talked about getting a professional birthing coach. She'd found three potential candidates from the website of Doula UK, but wanted Izzy to make the initial calls to contact them.

Izzy sighed. "Can't it wait? I've got a ton going on right now."

"I don't think it can wait. You're already, what, twenty-nine weeks along, and we need to make sure we hire someone. They probably can't take on that many clients each, and it'd be a good idea to at least make sure they're available."

Izzy threw her pen onto the bed. "I'm so sick of everybody telling me what to do. Izzy, do this, Izzy, do that. As if I magically have thirty hours every day. Are you sure it's necessary? Mum didn't seem impressed with the idea."

Eden leaned forward and touched Izzy's knee. She didn't blame her sister for being upset. "Yes, I think for you, a doula is necessary. Kieran and I will do our best, but, obviously, we don't have a clue about the practical things."

Izzy crossed her arms. "Really? I thought you were practically perfect in every way."

Eden frowned. "What do you mean by that?"

"You're the perfect businesswoman, perfect big sister and perfect Christian who's got her life all sorted out and can come and help her screwup of a little sister."

An icy wave chilled Eden's heart. "Is that really what you think of me? I'm very far from perfect. And you're not a screwup."

"That's not what people say. Some of the girls and women at church treat me as if I've got the plague. Apparently, sinful behavior is contagious." She sniffed and wiped her eyes with her sleeve.

Eden stood and walked around the bed. She sat next to Izzy and put an arm around her. "Let's get this straight once and for all. Everyone needs God's forgiveness. Everyone. There's not a single person who doesn't fall short in one way or another. You're no worse than anyone

else just because you stumbled in one area."

Eden's heart hammered as Izzy's head rested on her shoulder. Izzy thought Eden was perfect and was beating herself up. Eden needed to tell her the truth. She'd better do it now before she chickened out.

She sat up. "Izzy, I need to tell you something. I've made my share of massive blunders. You think I'm a perfect Christian? I'm not. I've... I've been with men. It didn't result in a baby, so it's made it easier for me to go around and act as if nothing has happened. But because your mistake is right up in front, literally, it's easy for people to point fingers at you and make themselves feel holier than thou."

Izzy stared at her, eyes round. "I had no idea."

"It was a while ago, and I've repented and been celibate for a while now. It's not something I go about announcing. I admit it, I've kept it a secret because I didn't want the judgment and finger-pointing. I'm too much of a coward to deal with that. You're very brave, Izzy."

Izzy hugged her back. "Thanks for telling me. I love you. You're the best big sister I could ever wish for."

The tight knot of fear in Eden's gut eased up. Her heart swelled.

Telling Izzy hadn't been that bad. Her sister didn't need her to be perfect. Izzy just needed her love and support. Maybe it would be okay to let someone else know, too.

Chapter Twenty

*E*DEN SLID a glance across at Noah as they walked out of the movie theater and into the brightly lit lobby. Over the last few weeks, she had seen little of him.

The TV production team were more interested in Izzy's academic prospects than her relationship with Kieran, and as a result didn't require him to be present much for filming. That meant Eden mainly

saw Noah at church, and they talked little beyond the usual pleasantries.

Finally, she'd asked him whether he wanted to watch a movie. Half expecting him to say no, she was delighted when he agreed. The film had been a hilarious romantic comedy. As they walked through the bright neon-lit theater lobby, Eden was reluctant for the evening to end.

As though reading her mind, Noah turned to face her. He pointed to a café on the other side of the lobby. "I'm feeling kind of hungry. Would you like to grab a snack?"

A warm fluttering filled her chest. They were going to spend some more time together. "I'd love some dessert."

The cafe was quiet, so it didn't take long for them to order and grab their snacks. They chose a corner booth.

Noah sank a fork into his chocolate cheesecake. "I don't think we've watched a movie together since we were what, seventeen?"

Eden nodded. "Yeah, that animated movie. Didn't we watch a matinée because the tickets were cheap and found the theater full of mothers and toddlers?"

"That's right," Noah said, smiling. "And they were all staring at us

wondering what we were up to in there."

"I'd forgotten about that. What movie was it, anyway? Was it one of the Toy Story ones? Toy Story 3?"

Noah's gaze drifted away. His smile withered. "It was Toy Story 3. I remember because I met Angela the next week, and she was taking her nieces to see it."

Eden was silent for a moment. "Wow, you remember the day you met her. I guess that's not surprising."

Noah shook his head, a small smile twisting his lips. "It sounds like a cliché, but it was love at first sight, at least for me. I was completely smitten."

Eden remembered that all too well. Noah had been so wrapped up in Angela that he noticed nothing else around him. "Yes, it all happened pretty fast. Why did you break up?" Rachel had already told her, but Eden wanted Noah's perspective.

He shrugged. "She didn't want to marry a pastor. She grew up a PK, you know, pastor's kid, so she'd seen that life from the inside out." His gaze wandered again, and he added quietly, "Like my mum."

Eden gave him a double take. What did his mother have to do

with it? She was just about to ask when Noah looked straight at her. "Where were you?"

A sudden chill expanded in her core, as though she'd been injected with liquid nitrogen.

Noah continued talking. "That breakup was brutal. I thought the world was over and didn't know how I was going to come out of it. I really needed my friends, but it was like you'd dropped off the face of the earth. Where were you?" he asked again.

Eden's mouth was dry. Sipping her coffee didn't help. Her first instinct was to deflect the question and avoid a reply. But as she looked into his eyes, her heart told her she owed him an honest answer.

Geoff had been right about how closed off and reserved she'd become, not letting anyone in. She needed to tell Noah the truth.

She took a deep breath. "I was dealing with a lot of stuff. I thought it was best that I stay away."

He frowned. "You could have just told me that. Weren't we friends? I thought we told each other everything. I would have understood. But you didn't answer any of my emails and you changed your phone number."

"I know." Eden swallowed down her fear. Her entire body had gone cold, but she was going to tell him. She looked down and shifted in her seat. "It'll take a while to explain. I don't know whether you remember I was tipped to get a place in Oxford. My grades were perfect. I had an admissions interview all set up, and all I needed was to do a decent job at presenting myself. I'd had coaching sessions to ensure I'd do well. Mum arranged those. Well, I botched the interview. I went in and looked at the interviewers and my mind went completely blank. So, I got up and just walked out."

Noah stared at her. "I had no idea. Why didn't you tell me?"

"I was going to tell you. But when I called, that's when you told me you were getting married to Angela." Eden took a deep breath. "I felt like I had nothing. Mum was on my case about failing the interview. And I couldn't stand to stay around and watch you getting closer to Angela and getting married because I had a huge crush on you."

The words were finally out. The secret she'd held back from him for years. The reason she'd shut him out of her life, the catalyst that had led to everything else. She forced her gaze up to meet his. He stared at her, his jaw hanging open.

Chapter Twenty-One

*N*OAH GAPED at Eden. Her words did not compute, so he repeated them back to her. "You had a crush on me?"

She smiled, a weak smile that didn't reach far enough to warm up her brown eyes. "I packed up and left and deleted your contact details because I thought it was best to make a clean break and not hear anything about your wedding.

That's why I never heard about you and Angela breaking up."

Noah shook his head. His world was teetering off balance again. This was Eden, his best friend, his chum. How could she have fallen for him?

She took a deep breath and blew it out. "That's not all, Noah. There's more."

He whipped his gaze back to her face. More? What else could there be?

She clasped her hands together. "I went to Bournemouth to study film. Nobody knew me there. I didn't want to be Eden Falconer from the telly, who'd managed to blunder my way out of an Oxford place. I didn't want to be a failure who nobody wanted. And I met a guy." Her voice cracked. "I won't give you all the details, but I thought I was in love and he told me I needed to prove it."

She dropped her gaze onto her hands. "So, I did what he wanted, but he dumped me anyway. And then I thought, well, I've already messed up so badly that not even God wants me. So, I might as well have fun."

Noah gripped his head in his hands. He didn't want to hear this. This wasn't his Eden talking. The Eden he knew was his best friend, one of the most committed Christians he knew. She didn't have secret crushes and go off and live the kind of lifestyle this stranger in front of him was alluding to.

She was still speaking, her voice almost a whisper. "I hooked up with a lot of guys. I knew it was wrong and I died a little every time I did it. But I told myself, at least they want me. Then one morning after I'd been out partying, I woke up in some guy's bed. He wanted me to leave because his girlfriend was coming over. He didn't even know my name."

A tear splashed onto her clenched hands. "And I didn't know

his. He shoved me out the back door into the alley where they kept their garbage. He was getting rid of me just like I was a piece of trash. I didn't even have my shoes on."

Rage flared hot inside Noah. His pulse raced. He knew guys like that, who were after just one thing. He'd heard enough disgusting locker room talk from guys bragging about their conquests. The thought of a man like that getting his hands on Eden, throwing her out of his house after using her, perhaps laughing at her, made his stomach turn.

Eden swiped a hand over her eyes, then looked up at him. "That's when I knew I couldn't go on like that. On the way back to my dorm, I passed by a church. The doors were open, and I went in. I just poured everything out to God. The pastor came by and we talked, and thanks to him and his wife, I got the support I needed and got my life back under control."

She pulled a paper napkin from the dispenser and blew her nose. "So, there you have it. That's why I can't talk to your young ladies. I told Izzy a few weeks ago, but apart from her, you're the only person I've told who used to know me... before."

He turned his gaze away and stared at the table. The silence stretched between them, each second weighing heavier than the last. His thoughts were too scattered to grasp any single coherent thread. Finally, he grabbed at what seemed to be the biggest one. "I had no idea you felt that way about me."

"Would it have made a difference if I'd told you how I felt?"

The tone of her voice added to the dread that was settling in the pit of his stomach like a lump of lead. He looked at her face, at those clear eyes that he thought had kept nothing hidden from him before. He sensed the answer she wanted to hear, but it wasn't one he could give. "No. It wouldn't have made a difference."

Her features twisted, and she sank lower in her seat. Did she still have feelings for him? The kindest thing to do was to let her down, to make it clear there was no future for them as anything more than friends. He cast around for the gentlest words to use. "I don't think I want to be in a relationship with anyone. It's just not on my radar right now."

She blinked quickly, then turned her gaze toward her clenched fists.

"But I'm really glad you're in my life again," he said, brushing her hand with his knuckles. "What you

told me about... About your time in Bournemouth doesn't change my opinion of you. I've missed having your friendship. Can we just make the most of that and be good friends?"

She looked up again, eyes wet with tears. "Thanks, Noah, but I can't. I decided to be honest with you, to lay it all out. I did the just good friends thing with you before. I don't think I can do that again. I'm sorry, but I know my limits." She stood up and took her coat and handbag off the chair. "Goodbye, Noah."

He stared at her. "I'm sorry."

Her eyes locked with his briefly before she turned her gaze away again. She slung her coat over her arm and walked out of the café.

Noah's chest tightened. He'd hurt her. And losing her friendship hurt him. But what else could he have said? Her admission came while he was still trying to cope with the full extent of his parents' struggles and the memories that brought about his own breakup with Angela. Love, right now, seemed to bring more pain and confusion than joy. It was safer to shut it out.

Chapter Twenty-Two

EDEN RESTRAINED her feet from breaking into a run as she rushed away from the table. She wanted to get away from that coffeehouse as fast as she could. Far away from Noah and his pity.

Too bad she couldn't outrun the ache in her heart. She'd thought she'd felt God's gentle nudging to be honest with Noah. She had taken that risk, had opened up to him about everything, and he had rejected her. Again. Except this time, it wasn't a rejection by default because he was in love with someone else. It was a point-blank rejection of her, of the heart she'd exposed to him.

She got to the parking lot. Rain splashed onto her face, cooling her hot cheeks and mingling with her tears. Even the sky knew how she felt. She punched her key fob. Noah's words came back to her. *I don't think I want to be in a relationship with anyone. It's just not on my radar right now.* That was just guy speak for when they weren't into you and didn't want to hurt you by saying it straight out. If he had re-

ally loved her, he would have made himself ready, no matter what else was going on.

She started the car and drove out onto the road. Her windshield wipers thunked a dull rhythm. Well, at least she knew. She wouldn't have to dangle on a faint thread of hope any longer. She'd been hoping ever since she'd realized he wasn't married anymore.

Certainty was a good thing. And now, she had a proper sense of closure. She had buried her hopes properly, had seen them sink into the grave, knowing for sure they were dead and gone. She also knew she was strong enough not to go off the rails again, seeking comfort and affection in dark and dangerous ways.

As soon as she'd seen Izzy safely through this pregnancy, she could go back to Essex, back to her life, and make a new start. She was good at new starts. She'd stay until the filming was over and make sure they came to some arrangement where she could see Izzy and the baby.

The gates swung open as she neared the Falconer home. As she pulled her car into the driveway, the front door opened and Elonora came rushing out into the pouring rain.

She hurried to the car and began speaking before Eden got out. "Is Isolde with you?" She peered past Eden into the car, squinting into the interior lit by the weak dome light.

Eden shook her head. "No, I haven't seen her all day." Elonora wrung her hands. Eden frowned. "Is something wrong?"

"She's missed a photo shoot to-day, an appointment with her mid-wife, and a session with her tutor." Elonora's voice shook. "Her phone is turned off and I don't know where she is."

Chapter Twenty-Three

EDEN WALKED away, the heels of her boots clicking against the tiles. Noah watched her go, wanting her to come back, but knowing it was impossible. They had drawn the lines in their relationship, and neither of them were willing to go across.

Telling her he didn't return her feelings had been like shooting Bambi. But what else could he have said? There was no possibility of any future. A relationship, mar-

riage, was not for him. His father was ten times the pastor and the man Noah would ever be. And yet even he had failed to keep his marriage together. What hope did Noah have?

Ten years from now, he didn't want to be in a floundering marriage, where what had once been love had simmered into resentment or indifference.

But he was going to miss Eden. He missed her already. Reconnecting with her after all these years had reminded him of just how special their friendship was. He'd never had a friend like her. They were on the same wavelength in a way he'd never been with Angela or Charlotte. It hurt to lose that friendship, but there was no alternative.

Even as he tried to rationalize what he'd done, a quiet, insistent voice whispered inside his heart. Did he really only feel friendship for Eden?

That morning many weeks ago when he'd held her in his arms, it had felt so natural and right to comfort her, to show her that no matter what her mother might say, Eden was a woman worth loving, worth treasuring. She deserved someone who could show her that. But it

couldn't be him. He didn't want to risk another failed relationship.

His phone buzzed, and he yanked it from his pocket. Was it Eden? He glanced at the caller ID. Kieran. He sighed before hitting the call accept button. "Hi."

Kieran's words tripped over themselves in their haste to come out. "Izzy's gone. No one knows where she is, and she's been missing all day. Mrs. Falconer called me, and she can't get a hold of her either. She's missed a bunch of appointments and it's just not like her to do that."

Noah stood. "Where are you? I'll meet you and we'll look for her together."

Kieran was waiting outside his house, huddled under an umbrella against the persistent shower. He jumped into Noah's car, slamming the door after him. His eyes were wide and his cheeks were flushed. "Thanks for coming, Pastor. We need to find her. She shouldn't be out on a night like this."

"No word from her, then?"

Kieran shook his head. "Nothing. She's offline from her social media as well." He pressed his hands together and bowed his head.

Noah said, "You've got the right idea. Let's pray before we do anything else. Lord, we're very worried about Izzy. Please keep her safe and bring her safely home. If it is your will, direct our steps so we can find her. Amen."

"Amen," Kieran echoed. He pressed his fingers against his eyes and cleared his throat.

Noah pulled his car onto the road. "Where do you think we should start looking?"

"If it wasn't raining, I'd have said the Centenary Park. She likes sitting out there, watching the ducks and swans."

"Maybe we ought to check. She might have gone there before the rain started."

Kieran nodded. "Okay, let's start there."

Noah drove a few minutes and came to the park entrance. He parked his car, and they both got out, each holding an umbrella.

They walked down the gravel path. The park was quiet, apart from one hardy soul fully decked out in rain gear and walking a dog. In a few minutes they got to the small lake in the center of the park. There was no one sitting on any of the benches, and no sign of Izzy.

Noah turned to Kieran. "It wasn't likely she'd be here, but at least we can rule this place out. Where else can we look?"

"Maybe the cinema? She could have been watching a movie."

Noah frowned. "I was just at Cineworld and didn't see her there, but it wouldn't hurt to ask if anyone spotted her."

Back at Noah's car, Kieran put his hand on the door handle. "What's that verse your dad keeps quoting? The one about how God hasn't given us the spirit of fear?"

Noah looked at him. "That's right. God has not given us the spirit of fear, but of power and of love, and of a sound mind."

Kieran nodded. "I've been trying to hold onto that verse. It seems I'm scared all the time."

Noah unlocked the car doors, and they put their umbrellas in the footwells. "Scared of what?"

Kieran shrugged. He slid into his seat. "Obviously I'm scared right now, worried about where Izzy's gone. But I'm scared about everything. I'm scared for the baby, whether it will be healthy. I'm scared about the birth, for how Izzy will come through it. I'm scared of what will happen afterward, of how

things will be between us. Whether we can keep going."

"I get it," Noah said. "There's a lot to be fearful about."

"Yeah. But then there's another verse that says perfect love casts out all fear, right?"

Noah started the engine. "That's right. 1 John 4:18." He quoted the familiar text. "There is no fear in love; but perfect love casteth out fear, because fear hath torment. He that feareth is not made perfect in love."

"Yeah, that's the one," Kieran said. "I'm not trying to say I'm a wonderful super Christian or any-thing. But that's how I feel. I'm scared every day. I'm afraid of messing up every day. But I still have to show up and do the right thing, especially if it involves some-one I love."

He looked at Noah. "If there's one thing I know for sure, it's that if you've got someone you love, you need to treasure them. You never know how long they'll be with you. I learned that when I was twelve. When I told my mother 'I love you,' I didn't know that was going to be the last time. I don't want to hold anything back, no matter how scared I am. Because I don't know how long I've got."

Noah concentrated on turning the car onto the road. Things look so simple when you're just seventeen. At that age, you think love can conquer everything and sort out every situation. Well, it couldn't. He knew that for a fact. He grunted a reply.

Chapter Twenty-Four

EDEN GRIPPED the inside door handle of her father's car as Gregory made another pass down the High Street. They'd been driving around for hours looking for Izzy while Elonora remained at home in case Izzy showed up.

Eden had called everyone she could think of. Now, the only thing left to do was wait and look.

Her gut churned. Where could Izzy be? Why had she taken off like

that? She turned to Gregory. "Has she ever done anything like this before?"

He shook his head, slowing the car down as they drove past a charity shop. Like all the other shops on the street, it was closed, shutters pulled down. "No, she's never disappeared like this before. Well, not counting the time she went to visit you without telling us. She's always been dependable and reliable."

"I should have noticed something. She's been under so much stress lately."

Gregory glanced at her. "Don't beat yourself up. You've been really good for her."

Eden's heart swelled. "Really? To hear Mum tell it, I ought not to have showed my face around here."

Gregory turned his car into a deserted supermarket parking lot and pulled to a stop. He sighed and looked at Eden. "Your mother says a lot of things, but she knows Izzy has handled everything a lot better because you're here."

An aching lump filled her throat. She swallowed hard. "Do you mean that?"

"Absolutely."

"Then why does she say the things she does?"

Gregory sighed. "You have to understand your mother. She really does want what's best for Izzy. For both of you. In her mind, the surest and quickest way to succeed is by having a big public platform which you can leverage into whatever other business you want to run. Being on reality shows is a crucial part of her business strategy."

Eden twisted a lock of hair around her finger. "I can understand that up to a point. A lot of people have used reality shows to launch their careers, but she's fixated on it as though being famous is the only path to success."

"Do you know much about your mother's upbringing?"

"No," Eden said. "I know she grew up in children's homes, but she's never talked much about it."

"Yes, she went into the care system at quite a young age. A long time ago, she opened up to me about what it was like. She told me she was bullied mercilessly. The one thing she remembered enjoying was watching Starsearch, seeing how all those unknown people would come on TV and become famous. She latched onto the idea that one day she'd be on television, get rich and famous, and show all those people she's not just a nobody. I think that's why she's so driven."

Eden remained silent. Not just driven. Elonora was obsessed with fame. But Gregory's words cast it in a new light. Her mother was wrong, but at least Eden had an inkling of understanding about the environment that had shaped her.

Gregory squeezed Eden's shoulder. "I've always regretted not stepping in more when you were growing up. You've had a tougher time than Izzy. But I felt I didn't have the right to interfere."

Tears stung Eden's eyes. He had tried his best, but he was her stepfather. "I understand. Thanks for telling me all this. It doesn't change the past, but it helps a lot."

Gregory started the engine. "For what it's worth, I'm very proud of what you've done with your life. You're a wonderful role model for your sister."

Eden swallowed hard. A tear rolled down her cheek.

Gregory patted her shoulder. "Come on. Let's keep looking."

Chapter Twenty-Five

A COUPLE OF hours later, Noah and Kieran were parked at a BP gas station, cups of takeaway coffee in hand. Noah glanced at the clock on his dashboard. 3AM. They'd been out for hours, searching for Izzy.

He rubbed his eyes. They were gritty with exhaustion. Although he wracked his mind, he couldn't think of anywhere else to look.

Eden must be sick with worry. His heart squeezed. After what he'd told her earlier tonight, now she had to go through this. For her sake, he prayed Izzy would turn up soon, safe and well.

Kieran sipped his coffee, then looked up at Noah. "Maybe we could take one more drive through the city center or the mall or somewhere?"

Noah suppressed a yawn. "We could do that, but I think it might be better if we call it a night. We're both exhausted and soon it won't be safe to drive anymore. We'll be able to help better if we get some rest."

Kieran looked down at his cup. "I know, but I just don't like to think of her out there somewhere."

Noah reached out and touched his shoulder. "I know. But we prayed and we've got to trust God. We'll not do Izzy any good by running ourselves completely into the ground. Let's catch a couple of hours' sleep and start looking again."

Kieran pushed his hand through his hair and nodded. "Okay."

Noah set his cup into the cupholder and started the engine. "You could crash at my place if you don't mind sleeping on the sofa. It'll be easier than going across town to your house. And it'll save us time when we start looking again tomorrow."

"Thanks. I'll send my uncle a text message to let him know."

Kieran touched the screen of his cell phone. As he did, it lit up and beeped. Kieran opened the text message, then sat up with a jolt. He looked at Noah, eyes bulging. "She's at McDonald's. My friend who works there said she's been sitting there all night."

"Which McDonald's?"

"The one at Station Square. I didn't think to look there." Kieran's voice cracked in his excitement.

Noah started the engine and made the ten-minute drive to Station Square.

Kieran was out of the car the instant it stopped. He rushed into the brightly lit restaurant. Noah followed. Izzy sat in a booth near the window, hunched over the table, hands wrapped around a large paper cup. She looked up, her gaze connecting with Kieran.

Kieran was by her side in a second, and the two melded in an embrace.

Noah walked forward. Izzy raised a tired, tear-streaked face and looked up at him. "Are you okay?" he asked.

She nodded. "Yeah."

He sat on a chair opposite her. "A lot of people are very worried about you. Why didn't you let someone know where you were?"

Her lips trembled, and she dropped her gaze. "I'm sorry. I just couldn't—it was all too much. Too many things to do, getting pulled in every direction. I had to get away."

"The most important thing is you're okay. Come on. Let's get you home."

Eden watched the clock, willing its hands to move faster. Gregory had gone to bed exhausted, telling

Eden to wake him in a couple of hours.

Elonora had called every person she could think of, but no one had seen Izzy. Now, she was on the phone to the police again, talking at the top of her voice. "This is a sixteen-year-old girl, a minor, who is thirty-seven weeks pregnant. She is a vulnerable, at-risk person and you're saying you can't do anything?" She paced up and down as a voice squawked from the handset.

Eden clasped her hands. "Dear Lord, please keep her safe and bring her back to us." She stood and went to the window, peering outside. Was there anything else she could do? Anywhere she could look, anyone else she could call?

Elonora spoke again. "Fine. That's more reasonable. Thank you. Good night." She lowered the phone and looked at Eden. "The police will send out a patrol car to drive around town. If Izzy doesn't show up by morning, they'll escalate."

Eden's phone buzzed. She glanced at it, heart thumping when she read the caller ID. Noah. Kieran had said he and Noah were searching for Izzy together. Had they found something? She opened the text message.

We found Izzy. She's been at Mc-Donald's all night. She's okay and we're bringing her home.

Eden sank onto the sofa, her knees weak with relief. *Thank you, Lord!* She looked up at Elonora. "Izzy's okay. Noah and Kieran found her, and they'll be here with her soon."

Elonora sat down, covering her face with her hands. "Thank God." She sat quietly for a moment, taking deep, slow breaths. Her face was drawn and tired when she spoke again. "I'd better send a message to the production team and her agent and let them know she's okay."

A searing wave of anger flooded through Eden, displacing her relief. "Is that all you can think of? The production team? What are you going to do? Turn this into a piece of on-screen drama? Your daughter has been missing and the first thing you think about is the TV show. Not Dad, not the police, not anyone else who's been worried sick about her."

Eden slammed a fist onto the sofa cushion with a force that shocked her and caused Elonora's eyes to widen. She stood, her pulse racing. "If this doesn't show you how wrongheaded you are, I don't know what will. You've been piling the pressure on Izzy. TV show, tutor,

entrance exams. What do you want to happen? Are you waiting for her to collapse?"

Elonora stared at her, mouth open. Gregory walked in, his hair rumpled, and stared at Eden. He stood next to Elonora and placed his arm around her shoulders. "What's going on here?"

Eden knew she was shouting, but she was beyond caring. "This was a wake-up call, Mum. If you won't protect her, if you won't put her first for once, I'm going to step in. I don't care what you do. You can sue me if you want, but there's going to be no more TV production and no more tutors or photoshoots or PR until this baby is safe and Izzy is okay. This was the absolute last straw. I mean it, Mum. It stops today."

"What's going on?" Gregory asked again. "Eden, I know we're all under a lot of stress. Let's calm down and deal rationally with whatever it is. Getting worked up won't help us find Izzy."

Elonora glared at her, her lips compressed in a thin line. She didn't reply but stalked out of the room.

Eden's legs felt like rubber. Her body was shaking. She sank into an armchair. "Izzy's safe. Noah and Kieran will get here with her any

minute. Maybe you'd better see to Mum."

Gregory stared at her for a moment, then followed in Elonora's trail.

The main gate buzzer rang and Eden heard Noah's car pulling into the driveway. She rushed to the front door and flung it open. Izzy climbed slowly out of the car. Eden rushed to her and hugged her tightly. "Are you okay?"

"Yes. I'm sorry for scaring everyone. I just wanted some space and didn't know how else to get it."

"I'm so glad you're okay." Eden choked up, tears blurring her vision. She looked up and her eyes met Noah's over Izzy's head. "Thank you," she whispered.

Noah nodded and stepped back into his car. Eden kept her arm around Izzy's shoulder as they walked toward the front door. "Thank you, Lord," she prayed silently.

There would be some fallout over her blowup with her mother. But they would deal with that tomorrow.

Izzy stiffened as they stood on the front doorstep. "Oh! I just felt something popping!" She stopped short, looking down at her tummy. At the same moment, a stream of

clear fluid gushed down her legs, forming a pool around her feet.

Chapter Twenty-Six

EDEN STARED at the pool of water gathering around Izzy's feet. "That's—you're—we need to call the hospital."

Izzy stared at her and nodded. "Okay."

Kieran rushed out of Noah's car. "Is the baby coming?"

Noah was out, too, his eyes wide.

"I think so," Eden said. "I'll—"

Elonora stepped into the doorway. Her gaze settled on Izzy and

she put an arm around her. "I'll call the hospital."

Eden tried to remember what she'd heard in the antenatal class and when she'd sat in on Izzy's meeting with her doula. Pad. She needed to get a pad. She rushed into the guest bathroom and grabbed a towel.

She handed it to Elonora then went upstairs and ransacked the cabinet, looking for the sanitary pads which she finally found right in front of her in the first of a dozen places she had looked. Grabbing them, she hurried back downstairs.

Izzy sat at the bottom of the stairs, clutching Kieran's hand.

Elonora, leaning on a banister, looked up at Eden, phone in hand. "The midwife says we should bring her to the hospital for a check."

"Okay. I'll just get her to put on these."

Two minutes later, they had sorted Izzy out with a fresh pair of underwear, dry tracksuit bottoms, and a sanitary pad, and were on their way to the hospital. In the bustle, Eden was dimly aware that Noah had said goodbye and faded away. She had barely registered him going. She was driving, and Elonora sat in the passenger seat with Izzy and Kieran in the back.

The maternity wing was quiet, and Izzy was ushered straight through to an exam room. Eden waited while Elonora went in with her daughter.

Kieran paced up and down, fists clenched, lips moving. At one moment he stopped and looked up at Eden. "I'm going to be a dad."

Eden smiled. "That's right."

Elonora and Izzy came back into the hallway.

Kieran rushed to Izzy's side. "What did the midwife say? Is the baby coming?"

Eden's heart squeezed at the expression on his face. There was not a single doubt in her mind that this boy loved her sister. She shot up a silent prayer to heaven that God would help them work things out somehow.

Izzy stared at Kieran, her eyes round. "The baby's coming. But the midwife says there's still quite a way to go. She said I should go home and try to get some rest."

Eden turned to Elonora. "Is it okay if Kieran stays over?"

Kieran's eyebrows flew up, and his gaze shot to Elonora. Elonora's jaw tightened. She glanced at Eden, then nodded. "Yes, that's fine."

They got back into the car and Eden drove them all to the Falcon-ers' home. While Izzy took a shower, Eden sorted out the guest bedroom for Kieran. "Thanks so much," he said, clutching onto the towel and toothbrush she gave him.

"No problem. Try to get some rest. Tomorrow will be a busy day."

Kieran yawned. "You'll tell me if anything happens, right? I don't want to miss a thing."

Eden smiled. He was absolutely adorable. "Of course. Good night."

Eden settled Izzy into her bed, prodding several pillows into place around her. "Are you sure you're okay? Are you getting any contractions?"

Izzy shifted a bit, then settled back onto her pillows. She swallowed hard. "A bit, but they're still okay." She squeezed Eden's hand. "I'm trying to remember what the doula said, but I'm still scared."

Eden squeezed her hand back. "I'll send her a text right now and let her know you're in labor. She said the best thing you can do is relax, right? Try to do that."

Eden messaged Anita the doula and although it was the middle of the night, a reply came in an instant. She looked up at Izzy. "Anita will be here in a couple of hours. She said to remember your breathing and relaxation exercises. Shall we try to do those?"

She talked Izzy through the relaxation techniques Anita had taught her as Izzy lay curled on her side, eyes closed. Eden stroked her hair. In the rush to get to the hospital they had not yet talked about what had happened today, why Izzy had gone AWOL. But that could all wait. "I'll turn the lights off now. Let me know if the contractions get stronger and more frequent, okay?"

"Okay," Izzy said, her eyes still closed. "Could you put on the rainy meadow noises?"

"Sure." Eden found the white noise app her sister was talking about and scrolled to Izzy's favorite rainy meadow. She turned her Bluetooth speaker on, and the sounds of a gentle rain shower and birdsong filled the air.

Eden turned the light off and settled onto a futon in the corner of the room. Her mind briefly touched on her talk with Noah. She pushed the thoughts firmly away, breathing through the physical pang of pain. Her heartbreak would pass. There was no point brooding over a man who didn't want her. She needed to stay focused and strong for Izzy. She settled down and closed her eyes with a prayer for Izzy.

Izzy's voice dragged Eden back from a dream. "Is the doula here yet?"

Eden sat up, instantly awake. "What's going on? Is the baby coming?"

"I'm not sure. The contractions seem stronger now." Izzy's hands rested on her bump.

Eden glanced at her watch. It was almost seven. She hadn't expected to sleep that late, even though it had been close to five when she'd gotten to bed. She grabbed her phone. A message had come through from Anita a couple of minutes ago. *On my way.*

Eden jumped up. "She said she's coming. She should be here pretty soon. Are you okay?"

Izzy nodded. She closed her eyes and took a long, slow breath, her fingers spread over her tummy. "I... can... handle it. I'll just try to keep relaxing."

Eden squeezed her shoulder, then went into the bathroom and splashed water onto her face. "I'll go downstairs and wait for Anita."

The house was quiet as Eden made her way to the front door. Elonora, Kieran, and Gregory must still be asleep. She breathed in the crisp morning air. The doula's car

pulled up to the gate and the security man buzzed her in.

Eden stepped forward as Anita got out of her car. Eden smiled at the sight of the short, plump woman. "I'm so glad you're here. Izzy seems okay, but I'm kind of worried."

Anita rubbed Eden's arm. "Don't worry. That's what I'm here for. Is Izzy still in bed?"

"Yes. She's awake but trying to relax."

Anita crinkled her brown eyes and squinted at Eden. "You look like you could use a bit more rest yourself. Here's the plan. I'll check on Izzy and you try to close your eyes for a while. I've had a good night's sleep, so I'll take over from here and let you know when anything needs to happen."

Eden smiled, the tension leaving her shoulders. "Thank you."

Izzy's face brightened when Anita walked into her bedroom. "Hi."

Anita grinned, squeezing Izzy's hand. "Someone's going to be a mum today. How are you feeling? A little scared? Don't worry. Your body knows exactly what to do. All you need to do is get out of the way and trust your body to do its work."

Eden headed back to her own bed as Anita talked to Izzy. Thank God

they'd hired a doula. Anita exuded calm, just like a diffuser spread perfume. She knew exactly what she was doing, and Izzy was in excellent hands.

A couple of hours later, Anita tapped on Eden's door. "I think we'd better head to the hospital. Izzy is an absolute champion. The contractions are about five minutes apart. She's in some pain now, but handling it really well, not panicking, remembering to breathe and relax. Who else is coming?"

Eden counted on her fingers. "Me, Kieran, Mum, and probably Dad."

"Shall I ride with you and Izzy and maybe dad-to-be?" Anita asked. "Will your mother want to ride with us, too?"

"I'll ask," Eden said.

A few minutes later, they all went to the hospital in a two-car convoy. Izzy groaned every time the car jolted, and Eden's entire existence focused on avoiding potholes and braking and accelerating smoothly.

Anita, Kieran and Elonora went into an examination room with Izzy, while Eden and Gregory waited outside.

A few minutes later, Anita popped her head out and spoke to Eden. "She's eight centimeters dilated. That amazing girl has done most of the work at home. It shouldn't be long now."

Gregory squeezed Eden's hand, then continued pacing up and down the room. The minutes crawled by, then the beautiful sound of a baby's cries filtered through the door.

Anita came out, grinning from ear to ear. "It's a boy."

"Can we go in?" Eden didn't wait for an answer but pushed past Anita into the birthing room. The midwife wrapped the child in a blanket and passed him over to Izzy. Izzy stared wide-eyed at the baby's scrunched up red face. She looked up at Kieran. He had dissolved into tears. Eden whispered a prayer of thanks.

Chapter Twenty-Seven

A COUPLE OF weeks later, on a sweltering hot day, Eden and her parents sat in the garden of the Falconer family home. The large umbrella was a welcome protection against the sun, but it was still hot in the shade.

Izzy and the baby had stayed one night at the hospital before returning home. She and Kieran had named the baby Adam Noah Haynes. "If it had been a girl, we'd have called her Eden," Izzy had said, stroking the baby's cheek.

Elonora tapped her lacquered nails on the glass tabletop, pulling Eden back to the present. "What is this about, Eden? I have things to do."

Eden sighed. The brief truce between her and her mother was long over, if it could have even been called a truce. Elonora had never referred to their conversation the night Izzy had gone missing, but the film crew and tutor had not come back. Izzy had had two weeks with nothing to interrupt her time with her new baby.

Eden said, "We're just waiting for Izzy. And there she is."

Izzy came out of the house holding a baby monitor. She looked relaxed in a loose cotton dress, her hair pulled back from her face, her feet bare. She shot a glance at Eden, and nodded as she sat down, setting the baby monitor on the table.

Eden said a quick prayer under her breath before she spoke. She looked at her mother and stepfather in turn. "Izzy and I have been talking and we think it's best that she and Adam move in with me."

Elonora sat bolt upright, her eyes shooting daggers at Eden. "What?"

Gregory put his hand on his wife's arm. He frowned at Eden. "Why do you think that?"

Eden was itching to speak but held herself back. This had to come from Izzy.

Izzy said, "I just think it would be the best place for us. We would be out of your way so you wouldn't have to put up with the disruption of a newborn in the house. Eden will help with childcare."

"And just how is Eden going to help with that? She has a job to keep up," Elonora said. "I've already picked a full-time nanny. You need to get back to school and carry on with all your plans."

"I haven't given up on school. But I don't what a nanny raising Adam, either. Eden and I will share the childcare. Kieran will step in, too."

Elonora stared at Eden. "So, you're following through on your threats. Is this your way of taking my daughter and grandson away from me?"

Eden shook her head. Brilliant. Now came the pity party with a healthy slice of guilt. "I'm not taking them far away. I put my flat in Basildon on the market and it's already sold. I'm looking for a property here in Hatbrook. You can see them whenever you like. This is just about giving them the space and the pressure free environment to grow up and figure out how their life is going to be. No one is trying to take Izzy or Adam away from you."

Izzy spoke up. "I'm a mum now, too. And I need to make decisions for Adam. I overheard you talking to your agent about doing a follow-up to the teen mums show. I don't want to do any of that. Staying here makes it so hard to say no."

Elonora rolled her eyes. "You make it sound as though I put a gun to your head and force you to do it."

Eden had to bite her lip to stop herself from answering. This was Izzy's fight.

"Of course, you don't do that," Izzy said. "But I just feel so guilty when you're talking every day about what a great opportunity it is and how other girls would kill for a chance like that and how hard you've worked to make it happen."

"But it is an excellent opportunity. It's a steppingstone to so much. Look what I've managed to build." Elonora swept her arm out, taking in the extensive garden and their home.

Izzy shook her head. "You've been very successful, but that path isn't something I chose. I never wanted that."

Elonora lifted her chin. "After all I've done for you, this is the thanks I get?"

Eden held herself back from rolling her own eyes. Elonora was pulling out every trick in the book. But laying on a guilt trip meant she must be running out of ammunition. Still, it was having an effect on Izzy.

Izzy's lip trembled, and tears filled her eyes. She reached out to touch Elonora's hand. "I'm very grateful for everything you've done for me, Mum. For all of us. But—" she could not continue and turned to Eden in mute appeal.

Eden spoke up, keeping her voice quiet. "You have done a lot for us. There's no question about that. But let Izzy and Adam have the space they need to figure out their own lives."

Elonora's eyes narrowed. "Figure out their own lives? You mean with you pulling the strings."

Gregory held his hand up. "Wait a minute, Elonora. I know this is hard, and I'll miss them, too, but maybe the girls have a point. Some space might be a good thing, at least for a while." He turned to Izzy. "You could try it for a few months, but you're always welcome to move back home."

Elonora looked at Gregory, then back at Izzy. She sighed and stood. "I can see you've made up your mind, so there's no use arguing. It's stupidly hot out here, and I've got some calls to make." She walked into the house.

Gregory squeezed Izzy's hand. "I love having you and Adam around, but I think it will be for the best that you stay with Eden. Your mother is about to sign on for a deal to shoot a series in Australia. We'll leave in a few weeks and will be away for quite some time. At least six months. I think this is a good idea on the whole, and good timing. I didn't really like the thought of

you being here with just a nanny. But we will miss you." He reached out and hugged Izzy.

Eden smiled. She couldn't avoid the cynical thought that this was why Elonora had conceded ground so quickly. She had expected a longer and tougher fight. But Izzy and Adam's moving out fit perfectly with Elonora's plans to film a new show, and the TV shows always came first with Elonora.

Whatever the reasons, Eden was grateful. Izzy and Adam would be coming to stay with her. "Thank you, Lord," she prayed quietly.

Chapter Twenty-Eight

NOAH SHOULD have been working. He had a stack of correspondence to go through, a sermon to prepare, and an assignment nearly due in a study course.

But instead of knuckling down and dealing with any of his pressing tasks, he was playing a mindless game app on his phone. One he wasn't even good at, judging from his losing streak. Once again, he failed to hit his points target and

the words "Too Bad!" flashed across his screen.

He set the phone screen down on his desk and pushed his hands into his hair. He needed to get a grip. Why couldn't he shake off this heavy cloud? Things were looking up with his parents. They'd found a marriage counselor they both connected with and were getting along better. They'd even been on a couple of dates.

And Mindy had finally stopped hanging around him. She'd taken up with a new church member, a widower with two young daughters. Supposedly, wedding bells would soon be ringing. So why wasn't Noah any happier?

He stood and walked to his bookshelf to grab a concordance he needed for his sermon. Running his fingers along the spines of the books, his hand rested on a small, tattered volume. It wasn't the one he wanted, but he pulled it out. *The Problem of Pain* by C.S. Lewis. He opened it, his gaze falling on the scrawled words on the title page. **To Noah. Sometimes life stinks. But God is still good. Read this, and let's talk**.

He gripped the book, staring at the words. Eden had given it to him when a friend of his had died in a

senseless and tragic way. Noah had been questioning his faith, wondering whether all the things he'd been taught about a loving and powerful God were true. He'd shared his doubts with Eden. She'd given him this book, and they'd spent many hours talking about why God allowed evil. She'd stood by him as he stumbled through that dark period. He'd come out with his faith restored, and he'd decided he wanted to become a youth pastor to help teens like his friend make better choices.

He slid the book back into its place. He missed Eden. Why did things have to be so complicated?

He went back to his desk, his hand reaching for his phone to attempt that level one last time before dealing with his email. A knock on the door arrested his hand, and he pushed the phone into his pocket.

"Come in," he said.

Kieran walked in, smiling. "Sorry for coming unannounced, pastor. Are you busy?"

Noah's mind flashed back to the first time Kieran had requested a talk with him. A lifetime ago. "Have a seat, Kieran. How's the baby doing?"

Kieran's smile widened into a grin as he settled into the chair. "He's just the greatest. He knows

me now and smiles when he sees me."

"Really? That's great! How about Izzy?"

"That's what I want to pick your brain about." Kieran leaned forward and cleared his throat. "I want to ask her to marry me."

Noah stared at him. "You want to get engaged?"

Kieran nodded. "I've been thinking and praying about it, but I want to know what you think."

Noah rubbed his chin. Why had Kieran come to him? He was the least qualified person to give marriage advice. Given the mess he had made with his own relationships, he didn't have a leg to stand on. But Kieran's eyes were on him, so he had to give an answer. "Let's have a quick prayer and we'll talk through it."

Kieran bowed his head, and Noah asked God to guide their discussion, give them wisdom, and make their path clear. As Kieran said amen, Noah sat back in his chair. He didn't have to give advice just yet. He could walk through the decision paths with Kieran and, God willing, the young man would figure out a decision on his own.

"Let's think about the pros and cons of you and Izzy getting married right now. Why do you want to marry her?"

Kieran smiled. "Because I love her. I want to spend the rest of my life with her and I want us to be a family and to be there for Adam."

"Those are excellent reasons. Anything else?"

"I want to show her that I'm committed to her, to us." Kieran's face flushed. "And unless we get married, it would be... would be wrong to—" his face turned a deeper shade of red. "To be together. You know. The way we were."

Noah nodded. He'd had the same struggle with Angela. He understood how hard it must be for these two to be celibate, given their raging hormones and their deep emotional connection. Desiring to fully express his love physically was a legitimate and biblical reason to marry.

"It's great that you want to live according to God's principles. So far, you're making a lot of sense. But let's talk about some reasons why it might be unwise to marry now."

Kieran frowned, but nodded.

Noah said, "You and Izzy are both incredibly young. I know you turned eighteen a few months ago."

"Yes. And she's seventeen now."

"Okay, so in just over a year, both of you will be over eighteen. Although you're technically an adult, you're still maturing emotionally. In fact, some scientists believe most people don't reach full mental maturity until they're twenty-five years old. In addition to that, you're both still financially dependent on your families."

Kieran's brows contracted together. "Yeah. Izzy and Adam are living with Eden, and her family takes care of pretty much all their expenses. And I'm still with my uncle." He sat up straight, his face brightening. "But I'm going to start an apprenticeship. My uncle's spoken to a friend of his who runs a gas engineering company, and they've offered me a place. I'll start next month, and I'll be able to train up to become a gas engineer. It'll take a little while, but I'll be able to support them."

"I'm glad you've got that arranged, but, yes, you won't be able to fully support them for a good while yet. And you have to think about your living arrangements as well. Where would you, Izzy, and the baby stay if you were married?"

Kieran slumped in his seat again. "That's a good question."

"And what about Izzy and her own career and education? Doesn't she want to go to university?"

Kieran nodded. "I wouldn't want to stand in her way. She's so brilliant and I would want to figure out a way for that to happen."

"So, that's another thing to work through. And, once again, since you're still dependent on others, you'd need to work it out not just between the two of you but between the people who are supporting you."

Kieran nodded, rubbing his chin.

Noah rested his elbows on his desk and steepled his fingers. "Your situation is a bit like closing the barn door after the horse has already bolted. We're very grateful for little Adam. His life is a blessing, not a mistake, and I know how much you, Izzy, and your families love him. But things have happened backward. That means there may not be a perfect solution. The Bible says when a man gets married, he should leave his father and his mother and cleave to his wife. The two are supposed to be one. They become a family unit, making decisions as one. But that's difficult for the two of you to do, since your decisions are being subsidized by other people. I'm sorry to be blunt,

Kieran, but you're an adult now, and I'm talking to you man to man."

Kieran nodded again.

Noah went on. "Getting married sounds like a good idea now, but you might grow resentful at having to run your decisions past Izzy's family. Can you handle that? I know it's a cliché about keeping your wife in the manner to which she has been accustomed. But, at least in the beginning, it will be hard for you to support Izzy and Adam and give them the things they've been used to having. Not without some help from either your family or hers. Again, would you be able to handle that? Without getting resentful?"

Kieran looked down at his hands. He remained silent.

Noah said, "I'm not bringing this up to be mean or to put you off marrying her. I love you both and I think you're great together. But you need to understand some of the extremely tough issues you'll be facing. These are things that have broken marriages between people who are far more mature than you and Izzy are. I'm not saying it's impossible, but the two of you will need a lot of support. We've already mentioned financial support, but you'll need spiritual support and help and

advice. Both of you must have teachable hearts and be open to listen to each other and to other people as well. Will you be ready to do that?"

Kieran looked at him, his eyes wide and clear. "Absolutely. I want this to work. I'll do anything I can to make it work. I know it's not perfect, but I want to try. I don't know how I could live with myself if I didn't try." He paused and took a deep breath. "I know I did things the wrong way around. But this is where we are now, and I want to do the right thing. Don't you think there's a way that Izzy, Adam and I could be together? Won't God make a way if we pray and do our best?"

Noah nodded. "I absolutely believe God can make a way. We just need to figure out what that way is so you can walk with wisdom. I'm very proud of you, Kieran. You've been amazing through this. Since that day you first came in here and told me about Izzy and the baby, I've seen you grow so much. I have no doubt that you love Izzy with the self-sacrificing love of a husband. And I think you have the heart and the maturity to make this work. But it won't be easy."

Kieran's eyes were misty as he smiled. "Thanks, Pastor. That means a lot to me."

"We'll figure out how to set up premarital counseling for the two of you when you go ahead and propose. You'll have a lot to work through, more than the average couple. I'd advise you not to set a date or make any firm wedding plans until you've had a few months of intensive counseling. But let's take a moment and pray."

When they were done with praying, they stood up, and Kieran reached out and hugged Noah over the desk.

Their eyes were moist when they stood apart. Kieran wiped his own eyes with his fingers. "Thanks, pastor. I'll speak to you soon."

Noah's throat ached, and it was a moment before he could reply. "See you soon. And congratulations. I know she'll say yes."

Kieran flashed a grin and walked out.

Noah sank into his chair, pushing his hands through his hair. He was such a hypocrite. He'd been assuring Kieran of how marriage required hard work and commitment, but Kieran could make it work if he relied on God's help and counsel from wiser people. He could dish

out the advice, but he couldn't take it for himself. This young boy, facing so many odds against him, was brave enough to make a go of putting together a life with the woman he loved.

Those words he'd told Kieran, why couldn't he believe them for himself? Why couldn't he accept that if he and a woman loved each other and were committed to each other, God could help them work through whatever challenges life might throw at them?

He'd stopped believing that when Angela split up with him. Then Charlotte had cheated on him. And his faith had taken another hit when he learned how deeply in trouble his parents' marriage was.

He'd told Eden marriage wasn't on his radar. That had been a lie. He thought about marriage a lot, but he was afraid. Not just afraid. Kieran was afraid. But he, Noah, was a coward. Even an eighteen-year-old was braver than he was.

He clenched and unclenched his fists. He'd been too much of a coward to face the truth that he loved Eden. It had been much easier to push her away, to avoid taking the risk and jumping out into the unknown. How could he be a pastor and not be willing to walk his talk? If he was going to tell people to step

out in faith, he needed to do the same thing himself.

Noah covered his face with his hands and prayed. He asked God to forgive him for giving into fear, and to help him fully open his heart to whatever plan He had in store.

Noah spent several minutes in prayer. When he finally lifted his tear-streaked face, he felt as though he'd been walking through his life with partial hearing and suddenly had his ears unblocked. Before, he'd been able to hear well enough to function, to survive. But now he was suddenly aware of a beautiful symphony that had been playing around him all along. Eden. Sweet, precious Eden, the dearest friend he'd ever had. Yes, he could exist without her: he had for many years. But how much sweeter, how much more depth and richness could there be in their lives if they walked together. If she would have him.

Chapter Twenty-Nine

EDEN HELD baby Adam close. She could never get enough of his delicious smell. Even when his diaper needed a change, like it probably did now. She smiled and walked over to the changing table, laying him on his back.

"Your timing stinks, little man. You waited just until I got you all dressed to go out, then you unleashed a poop. Let's have a look-see." She undressed him and checked his diaper, confirming her suspicions. "You've done a thorough job of it. Let's clean you up."

Adam squirmed and gave her a gummy grin. Her heart swelled. He was gorgeous, with Izzy's eyes and Kieran's smile. He was still bald, but he'd probably have brown hair like his dad. Perhaps the situation he was born in wasn't ideal, but he was here, and he was perfect, and she would do everything she could to help him have the best possible start in his life.

"That's right, little man. You are safe and you are loved. That's what matters most of all, and you've got that." She fastened a clean diaper

on, then blew a raspberry against his tummy. He squealed in delight, so she did it again.

Eden commuted to London three times a week, and she and Izzy had worked out a system that functioned reasonably well. Between the two of them and a lovely childminder who had been an absolute godsend, they took care of Adam without needing to put him in childcare.

Kieran had stepped up as well, spending every spare moment he could with his son when he wasn't busy with his new apprenticeship. Izzy was working hard on her A levels, with her eye firmly on applying to Oxford. And if that didn't pan out, there would be other options.

Life wasn't perfect, but there was a lot to be thankful for. And between her work and taking care of her unusual little family, Eden's days were full. She had little time to think about the things she didn't have, or brood over the ache in her heart when she saw Kieran and Izzy together.

Adam yawned as she picked him up. It was time for his nap. When the weather allowed it, she liked to put him in his buggy and go for a walk. He would sleep while she got some fresh air and dealt with some emails and admin work. It was Oc-

tober now, so any sunny warm day like today was a bonus. She slung her backpack over her shoulder and picked up Adam's nappy bag, looking around the room to make sure she had everything.

"Okay, little guy. Time to go."

The buggy was outside the front door, and she settled Adam down, tucking a soft blanket around him. She couldn't resist bending over to nuzzle his cheek.

She straightened up, and her heart dropped to her feet. Noah was standing on the sidewalk, watching her.

He walked up toward her. "Hi. Have I come at a bad time?"

Her voice came out as a croak. "I was just taking Adam out for a walk."

"Can I walk with you?"

Eden's heart hammered. Since that night at the cinema, she had barely exchanged a word with Noah beyond perfunctory civilities on the rare occasions their paths crossed. Why did he want to walk with her now? She nodded. "Sure." She checked the front door was locked, and they started down the sidewalk, heading for the Centenary Park, just a short walk from the house. They walked in silence for a while, Eden's thoughts too

fragmented and random to collect into sensible small talk.

They turned into the park gate. Noah looked at her. "So, how is it going with Izzy and the baby?"

"Good. I love having them with me."

"And how is Izzy getting on?"

Just social chitchat. She could do this. If only her stomach would stop fluttering like a herd of demented butterflies. Why was Noah here, though? She gripped the handle of the buggy tighter. "Izzy's great as well. She's going for four A Levels. She originally wanted to take five, but that's not practical with Adam."

Noah smiled. "She's exception-
ally gifted. I'm sure she'll be able to
handle it."

"Me too. Kieran's been fantastic
as well. He's really stepped up. He's
a very impressive young man."

Noah nodded. "He is. I've learned
a lot from him."

Eden shot him a look. "You
have?"

Noah nodded again. He pushed
his hands into his pockets, took a
deep breath and blew it out. "I've
learned from him that love is worth
taking a risk. I've learned that love
casts out fear. If you love someone,
you'll step out in faith, no matter
how afraid you are. He's taught me

that love means reaching out in faith and hope instead of closing off your heart and cowering in fear and hopelessness."

Eden's legs had forgotten how to walk. She stood still and stared at him. His eyes were fixed on hers. She swallowed. "He's wise beyond his years."

"He is."

They walked in silence for a while longer. The path branched off to a bench under a willow tree next to a pond. There was a bigger lake in the middle of the park, but Eden liked to come to this little pond. Swans and mallards drifted across the water. Eden glanced into the buggy. "Adam's asleep."

Noah gestured at the bench. "Do you want to sit down?"

She nodded, and they headed toward the bench. Eden checked Adam's blanket before sitting next to Noah. The willow branches screened them off from the path, as though they were in a private room, cut off from the rest of the world. She wiped her palms against the sides of her jeans.

Noah turned to look at her, an expression in his hazel eyes that sparked a flame of hope inside her, a flame she'd been sure was dead.

"Eden, I owe you an apology. You remember that day at the cinema?"

How could she forget the day her heart had been smashed into a thousand pieces? She nodded. "Yes."

"You told me you had feelings for me once. And I pushed you away."

She stared down at her hands. Her heart hammered so loudly she could hear it in her ears.

Noah cleared his throat. "You were brave enough to tell me a lot of things. You were honest with me, but I wasn't honest with you. I wasn't even honest with myself. Eden."

His fingers brushed her hand, and she looked at his face again, her breath catching in her throat.

"Eden," he said again, "I'm going to be as honest with you as you were with me. I'm in love with you. I have been for a long time, even though I didn't admit it to myself. You're the best friend I've ever had, the person I could always tell anything. All my dearest, happiest memories? They were made with you."

Her fingers intertwined with his, and she clung onto his hand. Warmth spread throughout her body.

He raised her hand to his chest, pressing it against his heart. Under her fingers, she felt its strong beat, racing as quickly as hers. He looked into her eyes again. "I should have asked you on a date, taken the time to woo you properly. But I didn't want to go one second longer without telling you how I feel about you."

Eden swallowed hard. She was desperate to believe him, but fear clawed at her heart. This was coming out of nowhere. He'd flat out rejected her. Could he really love her? It was too exquisitely good to be true, far beyond her wildest hopes. "Are you... Are you sure? You sounded so certain when you said you didn't want to be involved with anyone."

His face twisted, and he held her hand tighter. "Yes, I'm sure. I was a coward and a fool. You are the kindest, strongest, bravest woman I've ever met." His voice cracked, and he took a deep breath. "My whole heart is yours. I love you with everything I am."

She moved her hand up to his face, and he turned his head and kissed the hollow of her palm. He leaned toward her and found her lips, kissing her with a tenderness that melted her heart and brought tears to her eyes.

Her arms encircled him, and he held her close and whispered, his lips against her hair, "Do you still love me?"

"Always."

He tightened his embrace. "I'm sorry I wasn't there for you when you needed me. I let you down so badly."

"You didn't know. You couldn't have known, because I didn't tell you."

He pulled back, raising both hands to hold her face. "Just so it's one hundred percent clear, I don't care what happened in Bournemouth. That was never an issue for me. I know your heart. I know who you really are. And I love you."

Eden wanted to tell him she loved him, but her throat choked up. He was her best friend, and he knew her better than anyone else. She had told him her ugliest secrets, her deepest shame. She didn't have to wear a mask or hide behind a shield. He saw her, really saw her, and loved her.

He kissed her again, taking his time until she felt she would burst with joy.

Epilogue

Eighteen Months Later

EDEN CHECKED the small suitcase one last time. Socks, T-shirts, pants, a swimsuit, a couple of stuffed toys... Everything little Adam would need for a few days' visit with his grandmother.

She zipped the suitcase shut and wheeled it into the living room of her home. Elonora sat on the floor in the middle of an explosion of toys. Brightly colored building blocks, toy trucks and stuffed animals were strewn around her. Adam lay on his tummy, trundling a police car back and forth while Elonora gave a convincing impression of a siren.

Eden smiled. She would never have imagined her mother looking anything less than poised and stiffly elegant. But little Adam had done wonders for his grandmother. Izzy and Eden often laughed over how this tiny child had effortlessly flipped the "grandma switch" within Elonora. After several months filming in Australia, Elonora had returned to the UK and fallen head over heels for the boy. She had jumped at the chance to babysit him for the second week of Izzy and Kieran's honeymoon.

Eden patted the suitcase. "I think I've got everything in here. Most crucially, Snuggle Bunny."

Elonora looked up. "Did you remember to pack one of Izzy's sweaters for Adam to hold at bedtime? It was a lifesaver last time he slept over."

"Yes, I put one in there, too."

"Which one?" Elonora asked.

"The purple wool one with white flower thingies."

Elonora shook her head. "That's too rough. Get one of her cotton ones."

Hiding a grin, Eden grabbed a sweater from the hallway closet, choosing one that carried a whiff of Izzy's lavender perfume. She wedged the sweater inside the suitcase.

Elonora stood and straightened out her shirt. "Good. In that case, I'm ready to go." She looked down at Adam. "Shall we go, little guy? Ready to spend the week with Nana and Granddad?"

Adam sat up and fixed his large brown eyes on Elonora. "Go?"

Eden stepped forward. "Yes, darling. You're going in Nana's car now. Going to Nana's house."

The toddler got to his feet. "Nana's house! Take police car."

Elonora chuckled. "Of course you can bring your police car. And wait till you see the surprise Granddad has waiting. Shall we go?"

"Yeah!" He slipped his hand into Elonora's.

She looked up at Eden and reached for the suitcase. "Thanks. I'll call if anything comes up."

Eden walked them to the door. She didn't expect there would be any trouble. Since returning from Australia, Elonora had spent a lot of time with her grandson. This would be the second time Adam was sleeping over. Adam tugged at his grandmother's hand as they stood in the open doorway. Eden smiled. That was a good sign.

"Have fun," she said.

"We will." Elonora took a step outside and hesitated for a moment, then turned and looked at Eden. "He's a lovely child. You're all doing a fantastic job." She picked Adam up and settled him on her hip, then walked down the path, pulling the little suitcase behind her.

Eden stood in the doorway, a lump in her throat. Elonora seldom

gave compliments, and this one was particularly precious.

Eden went back into her house and went straight to her purse. She rummaged inside and brought out the pregnancy test she'd kept buried in there all day.

In the whirlwind of preparations for Izzy and Kieran's wedding, church commitments, and work, Eden hadn't even registered that she was late. It had finally dawned on her this morning, and she'd grabbed the test while on her morning walk with Adam. But she'd been so busy with Adam and work that she hadn't had time to take the test until now.

Her heart thumped as she opened the packaging and read through the instructions. She and Noah wanted children, of course, but in the ten months since their wedding, life had been so hectic that there hadn't been space to think about it.

Until last week, Izzy and Adam had been living with Noah and Eden. They'd tag-teamed childcare while Izzy studied biology at Oxford University. Izzy made the one-and-a-half-hour commute each way from Hatbrook. Thankfully, she could drive herself to the university now. Eden still worked with Ruby, spending about fifty percent of her work hours in London or on site with their clients. Noah had his hands full at Grace Community Church, and Kieran was making progress in his apprenticeship. It was a busy, crazy time for them all, but Eden loved every minute of her new life. In an unorthodox, all-hands-on-deck way, they were making it work, and Adam was an absolute delight.

Huge changes were on the way, though, since Izzy and Kieran had gotten married. When they came back from their honeymoon in Cornwall next week, they'd be setting up home in his uncle's house. Kieran's uncle was moving into an apartment closer to his workplace.

Noah and Eden would have their home to themselves, but Izzy would still need a lot of help with Adam while she continued with her studies. And now, would Eden have a baby of her own to look after?

Her hands trembled as she followed the instructions on the digital test. She placed the cap back onto the test wand and washed her hands. Now, all there was to do was wait for the three longest minutes of her life. She set a timer on her phone, then put it face down on the coffee table so she couldn't see the seconds ticking by.

She looked at the back of her phone. Had three minutes gone by yet? Of course not. The alarm would have buzzed. If she made a cup of tea, that would take her mind off the timer.

As she crossed the hallway, the front door opened and Noah came in, backpack slung over his shoulder. He grinned as he saw her. "You'll never guess what news I've got."

"What?"

"First things first, Mrs. Chaplin. I need to say hello to my wife." He pulled her toward him, and they shared a long kiss.

She smiled and stroked the hair at the nape of his neck. "Hello to you, too." They walked to the living room.

"Is Adam already gone?" Noah asked.

"Mum just left with him. So, tell me. What's your big news?"

He beamed as they sat on the sofa. "I got a call from Damon Williams, the youth pastor for New Life Church in London. He's pulling together the speaker roster for next year's Hearts Aflame youth convention. They watched the YouTube video of the talk you gave at our Spring into Life conference, and they want you to lead a session with the girls at Hearts Aflame next year."

Warmth rushed over Eden. Following a nudging in her heart, she'd agreed to speak to the teen girls at Grace Community Church, sharing about the mistakes she'd made in her own life and how God had restored her. On a last-minute whim, she and Noah had put the video of the talk on YouTube.

She'd been overwhelmed at how many girls and young women had reached out to her, responding in hope to her testimony. They needed to know they were precious daughters of the King and didn't need to cheapen themselves with men who didn't deserve them. And now she was being asked to speak at one of the UK's biggest events for Christian teens.

She pressed her hand against her heart. "Wow! I don't know what to say. That's huge! Do you think I should do it?"

He smiled. "You'd be absolutely amazing. But it's up to you if you want to. I told Damon you'd pray about it." The alarm on Eden's phone beeped, and Noah looked around. "What's that?"

Eden jumped up and cut off the alarm. "It's a reminder to check on something. Hang on."

She hurried to the bathroom and picked up the test wand. The words on the small digital display stood out in sharp, unmistakable clarity. Her body thrummed as though an electric current ran through it. She walked slowly back to the living room.

Noah watched her from the sofa, frowning. "Is everything okay?"

She held up the test. "It's positive."

His eyes widened, and he jumped to his feet. He was next to her in one bound, staring down at the test, then back into her face. He folded her in his arms, squeezing her tightly. When he finally spoke, his voice was husky. "After everything you've already done for me, you're making me a father, too?"

Her heart soared, riding high with the pure intensity of her love for him.

Finally, he stood back, wiping his eyes with his fingers. "I didn't think it was possible to be so happy."

She laughed. "I don't know how it happened."

He grinned. "Well, when a man and a woman love each other very much—"

Eden laughed again and punched his arm. "I mean, I've been so busy I hadn't even thought about it. It's going to be absolutely mad with work, church, and helping Izzy out with Adam."

He stroked her face. "We'll do what we've always done in our crazy, beautiful family. We'll all pull together and make it work."

She threw her arms around him. What had she ever done to deserve all this? God had blessed her so much, and her cup of joy overflowed. Noah was right. They would make it work.

The end

Get a free book

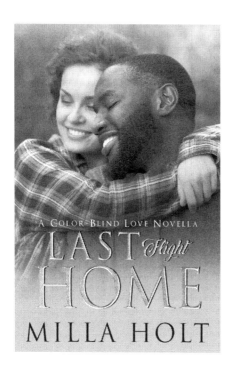

Dumping him was the right thing to do... Wasn't it?

Five years ago, Macey called off her engagement to the love of her life. She wasn't expecting to ever

see him again, or be stuck next to him on a transatlantic flight...

Caleb prides himself on doing the right thing, no matter what. He once made a choice that cost him the woman he loved. Now, when he's trying to make up his mind about a possible new relationship, he finds himself seated next to his lost love, Macey, for the next nine hours. Is it too late for him to find a way back into her heart? Should he even try?

Last Flight Home is FREE and not available in any stores. Find it on https://www.millaholt.com

About the Author

I write fiction that reflects my Christian faith. I love happy endings, heroes and heroines who discover sometimes hard but always vital truths, and stories that uplift and encourage.

My family and I live in the east of England where we enjoy rambling in the countryside, reading good books and making up silly lyrics to our favorite songs.

To learn about my other books, join my mailing list, and grab a free exclusive book, visit my website at www.millaholt.com

Printed in Great Britain
by Amazon